A Spirit of Steel . . . A Melting Heart

Juliana felt her body shiver, and she gathered the blanket around her. Instantly Nicholas was at her side.

"Are you truly well?"

"Quite," she replied. "I was merely . . . cold."

His eyes sparkled, and a gentle smile drifted over his face.

"Perhaps I can do something about that," he said and, wrapping his arms around her, pulled her to his chest. Juliana's gasp of protest died quickly as she felt the warmth surround her and heard the pounding of his heart.

Finally Juliana raised her head.

"Thank you for rescuing me, Nicholas," she said with a tentative smile.

He held her away from him and scrutinized her face. Suddenly he smiled mischievously.

" 'Twas the least I could do, Juliana, to return the favor of last night."

"I must go back and change out of my wet clothes," she said, averting her gaze from his.

Nicholas took her hands and helped her to her feet without a word. Slowly he brought her fingers to his mouth and caressed them with a slow, burning kiss. She stood motionless, staring. Finally he let her hands go.

"I would not want your chill to return, Juliana," he said softly, and moved aside to let her pass.

Noble Deception

Eileen Winwood

JOVE BOOKS, NEW YORK

NOBLE DECEPTION

A Jove Book / published by arrangement with
the author

PRINTING HISTORY
Jove edition / March 1992

ISBN: 0-515-10806-5

Jove Books are published by The Berkley Publishing Group,
200 Madison Avenue, New York, New York 10016.
The name "JOVE" and the "J" logo
are trademarks belonging to Jove Publications, Inc.

PRINTED IN THE UNITED STATES OF AMERICA

10 9 8 7 6 5 4 3 2 1

To Alan and Andy,
who make all things possible

1

Summer 1813

Some Cupid kills with arrows,
some with traps.
—SHAKESPEARE, *Much Ado About Nothing*

THE EARL OF PEMBROKE'S FROWN settled into a scowl as he surveyed the ancient French tavern which, it now appeared painfully clear, was his destination this night. The establishment bespoke a century, and the rotting oak door would offer scant protection against the rain. Regretting not for the first time the favor he had promised Sir James, the earl alighted from his hired nag and promptly stepped into an ankle-deep puddle.

"Damnation!"

Nicholas Framingham was a man of easy temperament and infinite patience. But he was not a man to suffer foolish errands, and this task had all the markings. He pushed open the door and instantly knew the worst of the evening was yet ahead.

A toothless old man held a pint on a table in the corner, and in the dim light the earl could make out a pair of cuts he charitably supposed to be smugglers. Nearby, a rowdy trio toasted each other. Nicholas's own French was passable, but he doubted there was an acceptable translation for their drunken tributes, especially as their ability to hold their spirits was surpassed by their enthusiasm for the task. As he hesitated in the doorway, the din gave way to silence.

At well over six feet, Lord Pembroke made a towering figure in the doorway. His hands, though slender, were massive and looked capable of inflicting substantial damage. His bushy eyebrows gave his craggy face an untamed look, and his unruly black hair conjured the image of a windswept pirate. His eyes were a smoky blue-grey reminiscent of a deep, rich pewter. Even more than his physical presence, his demeanor and the superior cut of his clothes marked him clearly as an aristocrat.

But those daunted by his fierce appearance had not the pleasure of knowing the earl. For Nicholas Framingham was at heart a peaceable man. In truth, he liked nothing so much as spending a rainy eve beside a cozy fire with his manuscripts. Lord Pembroke was a scholar, one of the breed who, while appreciative of the world's temporal delights, was nonetheless most happy to pursue the riches of the intellect, the fruits of its cumulative knowledge, and the rewards with which it imbued the spirit.

But he did not want for courage, nor were his eyes blinded to dangers such as he appeared likely to encounter this very night. Indeed, as to that he was awake upon every suit.

He doffed his great coat and settled with a studied nonchalance at a table near the door. Hoping his unknown contact would appear quickly, he mentally reviewed the secret code James had given him. Simply put, he felt ridiculous. Here he was, the eighth earl of Pembroke, sitting in a French alehouse and acting for all the world like a spy.

He was somewhere between Bologne and Ambleteuse, having followed James's instructions precisely, albeit reluctantly. His presence in France was on account of the armistice and Napoleon's grand gesture to demonstrate his dedication to peace by aiding the lofty cause of scholarship. The emperor had not only opened Paris to the annual meeting of classical scholars but had also promised safe passage home for each of the participants. Nicholas was not so immersed in his manuscripts that he did not suspect the little Corsican of playing a deep game. Still, he had felt fortunate in these times to spend a fortnight in Paris enjoying his field's best minds. Indeed, he had been more than pleased at the reception his peers had extended to his latest Aristotelian text.

Although there were only a token number of French troops along the French coast, owing to Napoleon's preoccupation with Spain and the Elbe, Nicholas was happy to have the emperor's papers speeding his passage to Calais for the crossing home.

The earl sighed. If only Calais were the end of it. James had seen an ideal opportunity to have Nicholas carry a packet from Paris to this godforsaken place, forcing the earl to extend his journey by more than a dozen miles.

It had sounded a simple matter to play the messenger, but the earl's conviction that James would be loath to involve him in anything untoward faded with each moment.

A crash of thunder startled the earl from his musings, and he looked up to find a barmaid standing before his table. Her ragged frock was filthy, her apron covered with stains. Smudges on her face made it appear as though she had just crawled out of a chimney. In the candlelight, he could see only her green eyes distinctly. She appeared to be leering at him. Her hair, which an English lady would have tamed into a glistening russet mane, hung down in matted tangles. In another setting she might have been made to be attractive. But here she merely fit in supremely with the surroundings. Speaking loudly and rapidly in French, she gestured to him.

"An English gentleman has graced our establishment?

Surely he must be lost this night. He cannot have journeyed all this way simply to sample Michele's cooking!" she teased, as the room erupted in laughter.

Nicholas frowned. The wench clearly saw him as the evening's entertainment.

She hitched up her skirt to reveal a bit of ankle and made a mock curtsy.

"And what may I bring you, my fine *monsieur*? Ale for your thirst or some other delicacy for your discriminating tastes? Surely a man of your bearing can afford the best. We have not much, but we will try to please you." The earl shifted uneasily. The others were enjoying seeing the English nobleman put to sport, and he wondered if it would be wise to remain.

Perhaps he could mark time by playing along with her game.

"As it was such a nice night, I could not resist a ride. Surely you would not begrudge an evening's outing," he replied in his acceptable French, sweetening the sarcasm with a smile as he casually brushed the rain from his coat.

The toothless man raised his eyebrows. The two smugglers studied him with interest.

"And right you are, *m'sieur*. It is a splendid night. Perhaps you will let me show you around our humble inn. A working girl doesn't often get a chance to feather her purse with English gold," the woman said with a broad wink.

Jeers and shouts of laughter filled the room. There could be no mistaking the girl's meaning. She looked at him archly. Nicholas felt his stomach tighten. To reject the woman's blatant invitation would cause a scene, and he did not relish the consequences of inciting this crowd. He should remove himself from this unsavory hellhole. But what of his contact? He could not leave just yet.

At his silence, the woman laughed and boldly sat in his lap.

"Come, *m'sieur*. The rain is stopping. Perhaps we can catch sight of the moon. The French moon, you know, is the most beautiful sight in the world," she purred.

The group was applauding lustily, but the earl heard only the woman's last words. He stared. It was the code.

"Did not you hear me?" she said, pulling him up and putting an arm around his waist. "The French moon is the most beautiful sight in the world. But we will miss it if you do not hurry." She handed him his coat and turned to the room with a flourish of her hand. "There, you see? *L'Anglais* is not so terrible."

She gave him an exaggerated, mocking curtsy and gestured to the door. The moment they were outside, he turned to her, his patience beginning to take its leave. "What the devil!" he began, but she put her finger on his lips.

"Kiss me, you idiot," she whispered in English. "Do you not see that we have an audience?"

Nicholas looked up to see several of the tavern's patrons watching them from the doorway.

The woman wrapped her arms around him and raised her lips. Her kiss was sweet and inviting as she pressed into him. The earl's involuntary reaction was immediate, for Nicholas was by no means immune to such charms, brazen though they were.

He folded her body against his. Nicholas heard what sounded like a drunken cheer just as he felt the gentle probing of her tongue. The strumpet was seducing him in front of the entire tavern, he thought dimly. But she was also drawing a response. He no longer noticed the drops of rain that fell gently on them. All he knew was her deepening kiss, the softness of her lips, and her breasts pressing against his chest. He felt the woman tremble, and he clasped her roughly to his body. Rather than being put off by her wantonness, he found himself drawn to her in utter fascination.

The door slammed shut, leaving them alone in the court-
yard. The woman held him a moment longer, then pushed
her arms up to separate them.

"We must go. There is not much time," she said, rustling
her skirts as she started through the stableyard.

The earl's reverie evaporated just as a raindrop made its
way down his nose.

"Who are you," he demanded, "and just what was that
charade?"

The woman turned. It was dark, but he could see that she
was not much above twenty. Her worldly performance in
the tavern had made her seem much older. Now, though,
she looked like a bedraggled young girl. Her face remained
obscured by the shadows.

"You are Sir James's friend, are you not?" she whispered,
again in English.

"Yes," he replied, "but I fear you have the advantage. I
collect that you are the person I was to meet in this infernal
place. But my instructions were to leave a package and return
the way I came."

"You are bound home to England?" she asked.

"Yes."

"Then you must come with me. The way you came is filled
with Napoleon's soldiers. The man who gave you the packet
has been killed. They are looking for you."

"And I suppose your friends back there will take great
pleasure in recalling our presence for the first soldier who
comes along, thanks to that little scene you created," he
said.

The woman approached a big bay as the earl's waiting
horse blew impatiently.

"They do not like the soldiers any more than I do." She
shrugged. "And they know me. At all events, it is the more
reason for us to make haste."

The earl's eyes narrowed as he assessed the situation. A

slip of a tavernmaid seemed an unlikely rescuer. Probably she would lead him to an ambush. On the other hand, he mused as he studied her deft preparation of her mount, she appeared to be a most unusual woman.

She swung up on her horse unassisted, sitting easily astride.

"Are you coming?" she asked, looking down at his nag. "Though I cannot say that horse of yours has much to offer."

The rain had begun again, showing signs of turning into a veritable downpour, the earl noticed.

"It seems the choices are rather limited tonight," he said with a sigh.

She rode like an angel. He had never seen a female sit a horse quite like that. Despite the now driving rain, she was effortlessly at home astride the saddle. The huge bay pounded his forelegs into the muddy road as the earl tried to keep up on the inferior mount he had taken from the posting house in Calais, thinking at the time that it was superior to a carriage for his clandestine errand. The woman's legs, exposed from under her tangled skirts, pressed against horseflesh like the animal's second skin. She moved as one with the bay, holding herself alert, always watching. She glanced back at him occasionally, willing his horse to move faster. The night closed around them as they rode silently toward the sea.

Nicholas fell into the woman's rhythm, losing his own sense of time. There were few men he would have followed into the unknown perils of the French coastline. Most females of his acquaintance would no more consider dashing about on a country road in a downpour than they would consider missing a London Season.

Despite his predicament, he smiled.

The jarring of the boat woke Nicholas abruptly. For a moment he could not fathom where he was. Then he remembered. A bobbing fishing boat bound for England on what

surely was not a fortuitous night for such transit. His head
rested on a curled damp rope that was the only pillow he had
been able to devise, and his head ached from the experience.
As the sea tossed the pitching craft, Nicholas surveyed the
crude cabin that served as his resting place this night. It was
then he remembered that he was not alone.

The woman lay nearby on the simple bunk, one hand
thrown over her face in a gesture of abject weariness. She
appeared to be asleep. Although Nicholas could not see her
face in the darkness, she seemed to be even younger and
more vulnerable than he had surmised. Her rough cloak was
wrapped around her thin body, and there was an air of fra-
gility about her in sleep that had not been apparent during
their pell-mell ride hours ago.

Nor had she seemed fragile when she led him in a scramble
down the foam-lashed rocks to a waiting dingy and the silent,
gnarled seaman who Nicholas was certain would be their
Charon. For the earl had no faith that the beaten fishing
vessel waiting offshore would bear them safely across the
channel.

He had a dim memory of callused hands pulling them on
board before they both collapsed, exhausted, in the boat's
belly. Then blackness.

As he gingerly pulled himself to a sitting position, Nicholas
studied the girl's reclining figure. What manner of female
would embroil herself in such a dangerous adventure? That
she was a spy he did not doubt. From all appearances, she
was on the British side. But what would possess Sir James to
pull such a woman into his net of secret agents? Nicholas now
knew with chagrin that his old friend was no mere diplomat
and in fact had used him shamelessly. He vowed to pay a
call on the baronet at his earliest opportunity.

But what of the chit? Had James forced her to betray
her country, or for that matter was she even French? Her
English, what little she had employed with him, was flawless.

Nicholas sighed. This night was becoming quite a coil.

He became aware that the object of his musings was unusually still, and suddenly he knew she was awake, too.

"Our accommodations are not perhaps of the first stare, but a welcome change from bumping along on horseback in the rain, do you not agree?" he said, making his voice convey the smile he hoped would draw the young woman from her stillness.

Silence.

"I do not believe we have made each other's acquaintance. I am Nicholas Framingham, Earl of Pembroke."

More silence.

"At the risk of seeming impertinent, may I point out that you now have the advantage of me?"

There was not a sound from the bunk.

Nicholas sighed again. Perhaps her English did not serve, after all. Or perhaps she was sensible of their singularly compromising situation and intended simply to say nothing for the length of this bizarre journey. He could not believe she was frightened of him. She had seemed to be made of sterner stuff. He would have to dust off his French and try again.

"*Je suis Nicholas Framingham*," he began.

"I know perfectly well who you are," came a voice in perfect English.

Nicholas pondered that.

"Then, as I pointed out earlier, you do indeed have the advantage," he noted.

Silence. After a moment, the voice said quietly, "Marie. I am Marie."

"Miss . . . Marie, I am delighted to make your acquaintance," he said, and thought he heard a muffled giggle.

Nicholas stretched out his cramped legs. Without being able to see his boots, he knew his burnished Hessians were ruined. Furthermore, he was quite sure the rest of his apparel would be deemed unwearable after this, much to his valet's dismay. Nevertheless, the earl knew he would not trade this night for a closet full of Weston's best.

"At the risk of seeming too familiar, may I inquire whether this type of . . . activity is your usual thing?" Nicholas asked.

The bunk was silent.

"I myself go in for tamer pursuits. Give me an excellent Aristotelian text and I am happy to sit for hours, poring over the master's prose."

As he expected, the woman said nothing. Nicholas smiled encouragingly and continued to prattle on.

"Much of my time is spent in my study refining translations or on expeditions searching for undiscovered Greek manuscripts. At present I am compiling a text to add to the existing body of work and debate. It is a narrow field, to be sure, but an intensely rewarding one.

"Aristotle had the right of it, you know, about so many things," the earl continued. "He said that to learn gives the liveliest pleasure, not only to philosophers but to men in general. Thus I find it most pleasurable myself to uncover the wisdom of antiquity."

The woman by now had sat upright and was staring at him with undisguised amusement.

"Surely it follows," Nicholas added with a twinkle, "that it is not an untoward thing to wish to learn more about one's traveling companions."

The woman laughed.

"Indeed, my lord, though one's wishes are often thwarted by the contrariness of others, to be sure. Do you not think it would be an uninteresting world if one's every desire were granted?" she replied.

Nicholas mulled that over with silent glee. So the lass had a brain and a sense of humor, for all of her aura of mystery. Well, perhaps he would learn something of her yet.

"As to that, I cannot say, of course. Still, it seems a small thing to pose simple questions and a singularly cruel whim to deprive an earnest scholar of his need to know," he said.

The woman gave him a look that, as best he could make out in the darkness, was grave.

"It is not a whim, my lord, to keep my own counsel. As you must have surmised, this is a dangerous enterprise played for high stakes. It is not a game, after all, nor a scholarly exercise. My name, and indeed my business, must remain my own."

Nicholas allowed himself a prolonged, wounded silence. When the moments stretched to minutes, the woman stirred again.

"I can tell you only that these"—she fiercely clutched the documents he had given her after their ride—"will save lives and eventually perhaps a nation. As for me, I believe it was another Greek who said that appearances often are deceiving," she continued, her eyes averted. "I have my own reasons for embroiling myself in what is without doubt a difficult arrangement. I have not always lived thus, but I can say that it seems like an eternity."

With that the woman lay back on the bunk. She did not speak again. Nicholas studied her. That she was beautiful, he suddenly knew of a certain, despite the smudged face that he could only make out in profile. He was beginning to think she had a beauty of spirit as well.

And he knew with an unexpected sense of dread that he would lose her once they reached England's shores.

2

He that is more than a youth, is not for me,
and he that is less than a man, I am not for him:
therefore I will even take sixpence in earnest
from the bearward and lead his apes into hell.
—SHAKESPEARE, *Much Ado About Nothing*

LADY JULIANA WESTLAKE frowned as she studied the column of figures on her desk, deepening the furrow in her brow and causing a crease to be etched between her eyes. Absentmindedly she rubbed the bridge of her nose where a pair of spectacles perched precariously. A cap, whose job it was to restrain a mop of curling auburn tresses, sat unevenly on her bowed head. Her gown of biscuit lawn was rather untidily wrinkled. That it was becoming more so as she wrapped her legs around the chair in concentration was clearly of no import to the wearer.

So immersed in her work was Lady Juliana that she failed to mark the arrival of Lady Emmaline Hereford, a personage whose entry into any room was a decidedly noticeable event. The countess was a rather large woman to whom middle age had been more than kind. She was still possessed of a pleasing countenance, her face given to repose in a beatific expression that belied the impatient and determined mind that raced within. With her girth and preference for embellishing fashion rather than simplifying it, she stood out at any function like a never-faded amaranth. This was particularly so as she favored the brilliant pinks and purples of the past decade.

Lady Hereford swept into the library in a rustling pink-purple taffeta and paused to observe her only niece deep in concentration.

"Juliana, if there is a less prepossessing gown in your wardrobe, I have not seen it. Where did you get that cap—from your abigail? And must you wear those off-putting spectacles? Why, I myself have never been able to see small work and have not felt it a great deficiency!"

Lady Juliana fought off her irritation, folded her ledger with resignation, and pushed back her chair to welcome Lady Hereford with a forced smile. She had long since discovered that those who prized appearances above all things could not tolerate her own apparent indifference to the matter. To debate the question, she had found, was seldom worth the effort. At all events, she was certain her aunt had something else in mind altogether.

"Was there something particular, Aunt, that you wished to see me about?"

"It is Sarah, of course, as you would see if you ever pulled your nose out of those accounts. The squire's son—the eldest, you know, but still a mere calf—is becoming too marked in his attentions. To be plain, Juliana, I fear my daughter in danger of making much of a simple country flirtation."

Wringing her hands in agitation, the countess shook her head, jeopardizing the fate of a curled pink ostrich plume perched precariously in her silvering hair.

"If she had but turned seventeen this spring, I would have taken her to London for the Season, of course, but she had the misfortune to be born in August!"

"Most unfortunate," Juliana agreed, her mouth twitching.

"Nothing for it but to take her for the Little Season, but I must find some manner of diverting her interest in the young swain for a few more months."

"I have always thought Nathaniel an admirable young man, Aunt. Squire is well-fixed, moreover. And his son's attentions to Sarah have been all that is proper, I believe."

Lady Hereford collapsed into an overstuffed chair with an angry flounce. She fixed her niece with a scornful glare.

"May I remind you, Juliana, she is the daughter of an earl and may look as high as she chooses for a husband? I have no desire to see her shackled to a country bumpkin."

"Now, Aunt, you must know that I count myself a country bumpkin," Juliana said with a wry smile. "For I much prefer Lindenwood and the Sussex countryside to anything the town has to offer."

But one look at her aunt's mutinous expression told her Lady Hereford was unmoved. Juliana braced herself for the worst.

"What do you propose, ma'am?" she said, not really wanting to hear the answer.

"Well, but we must give a ball, don't you know, and let Sarah see the array of young gentlemen eager to try for her hand!" the countess pronounced with a sweep of her arm. "Pity the country is rather thin of company just now, but we shall come about nevertheless."

Juliana looked at her aunt curiously.

"Why, what an interesting idea, Aunt, but do you not think Sarah is rather young to have a ball thrown in her honor?"

"Juliana, you ninny! Indeed so! It will be in *your* honor, of course!" She smiled in satisfaction.

Juliana paled.

"Me, Aunt? T'would be most unseemly! I cannot allow it!" Juliana shook her head, rose from her chair and began to pace, a habit her aunt had come to find most annoying.

Lady Hereford sighed wearily.

"Juliana, you cannot continue to shut yourself up in this drafty hole! You are all but past your prayers, and you know you cannot live here alone unchaperoned forever. Indeed, I cannot think what my nephew is about, disappearing for months on end, leaving things so unattended. It is fortunate Edward was able to spare me for an extended visit. But even I cannot rusticate endlessly. You must think of your future!"

With that the countess rose, arranged her skirts artfully and prepared to leave, the matter apparently settled. But Juliana stayed her hand. She was a full head taller than her aunt but so slim as to be eclipsed by the older woman's girth. Still, her touch was firm, and she spoke with a quiet authority.

"Aunt, your concern is touching, but I hardly think I need a chaperon in my brother's house," she said. "You forget this is my home, too. I grew up here. Though much has changed since then, to be sure."

Juliana turned to mask her rising anger, though whether it was provoked by her aunt or by the events of the past she could not have said. She had, on more than a few unhappy occasions in recent years, learned that allowing one's emotions undue sway led only to pain. The loss of her beloved parents had been almost too much to bear. And her brother— but that did not bear mention! And so Juliana had vowed to keep a tight rein on her feelings. Indeed, for the nonce, she knew she must! But the effort was sometimes overwhelming, she acknowledged to herself in her most candid moments. Now her aunt dared to talk of marriage! As if such a thing were thinkable!

In truth, Juliana knew herself much relieved, rather than distressed, at the absence of occasions in which to mingle with society and attract the notice of the *ton*'s most eligible bachelors. Her shunning of society was quite deliberate, her avoidance of the gentlemen equally so. Still, as she stared out the window, Juliana trembled slightly, recalling a pair of bushy eyebrows atop glinting blue-grey eyes that appeared unbidden before her mind's eye. It was a face that had drifted through her dreams for more than a fortnight, as did the memories of one passionate and entirely shocking kiss that had touched her very soul.

Juliana forced her eyes to focus on the scene framed by the window, as Lindenwood stretched before her in all its vastness, rolling up and down gentle hills and through thick woods before arriving finally at the sea. Here, at least for the moment, was peace. And in the calm of this day, there was no oversized lord to haunt her dreams.

Lady Hereford mistook her niece's silence for sadness and smiled tenderly as her own eyes misted over. She patted Juliana's shoulder.

"I know your parents' accident was a terrible ordeal, my child. My brother and your mother were dear to me, as well you know. But it has been six years—and just when you would have had a Season too, more's the pity! You are nearly twenty-four. Can you not look ahead, dearest, rather than dwell on the past?"

Juliana turned, her head erect as she addressed her aunt with composure. Her eyes glinted, but not from tears.

"You must stay here as long as you see fit, Aunt, but I beg you not to trouble about my future. I have no wish to marry, you know, and will not count it as a loss to remain unwed."

"Not marry! Why, Juliana, never say so. You have both fortune and beauty—if you would but trouble about your appearance, my dear—and could have your pick of suitors despite your age!"

"It is not my wish to place my fortune and person in any man's possession, ma'am. My brother and I rub along tolerably, and I see no reason why we should not continue."

Lady Hereford touched Juliana's arm. "But, my dear, what if some day Robert should marry? His wife may have other wishes."

Juliana said nothing and returned to the perusal of her beloved vista. The countess threw up her hands and spoke, this time more loudly.

"Pish! Marriage is not such a reprehensible state, Juliana. People have been known to grow beyond mere tolerance. Although my own marriage was arranged, Edward and I would be lost without each other if truth be told. And your dear father cherished your mother to his last breath. If there was a happier union, I have not seen it."

Juliana's rigid features softened then, and she turned to gather Lady Hereford's considerable bulk in a warm affectionate hug.

"I know, dearest, that you and Uncle Edward have been blessed, as my own parents were," she said with a smile. "But I despair of being so fortunate as to attain such a state myself. And I could not tolerate a marriage not founded on love."

"But you must give yourself a chance, Juliana, to find the right man. It will come, I assure you," Lady Hereford insisted.

"Would that I had your faith, Aunt," Juliana said and promptly found herself nearly toppled by her aunt's tearful and overwhelming embrace.

Into this moment intruded Barton, who had long since conquered any inclination to be surprised by what transpired in this vast house. Since Lady Hereford and her daughter had arrived, moreover, he had walked into many scenes where ladies had turned into watering pots. So it was with all the impassiveness of the superbly trained and long-suffering servant that he cleared his throat and made his announcement.

"Pardon me, my lady, Your Ladyship, but there is a caller—a Lord Pembroke," he intoned.

The august butler's news was met by a loud thump and a cry as Juliana broke from her aunt's embrace, inadvertently smashing one of her willowy hands into a vase. As Juliana reached to try to save it, she tripped over a table leg and nearly went sprawling on the Aubusson carpet. Barton moved quickly to help his mistress, who was standing inelegantly on one foot and grasping a bruised shin. The vase lay about them in shards.

"Juliana, really, I must conclude your deportment lessons were sadly deficient," the countess said, her eyebrows raised. "Now, Pembroke is it? Do we know him, Barton?"

"I believe, Your Ladyship, that His Lordship is in residence at Seagate," Barton offered as he steadied Lady Juliana and cast a mournful eye on the vase.

"Seagate! But it has been vacant for years!" Juliana cried.

Lady Hereford's brow cleared. "Of course! Seagate was Lucinda Cromley's home before her marriage to—some wealthy earl, I believe. Oh, whom did she marry?"

"My father, ma'am, Gerald Framingham, the seventh Earl of Pembroke," came an amused voice from the doorway.

Juliana looked up with a start into the twinkling blue eyes of Nicholas Framingham, who was studying the group with an interested smile.

The ladies stared at him, as much stunned by the man as by the disruption, for he dwarfed the sedate furnishings of the library. Juliana was speechless as she gazed up into eyes so blue-grey that they appeared smoky. Her dream, she realized with dawning horror, had become a nightmare. If he recognized her, all was lost!

"I apologize, ladies, for intruding into the sanctum of your library. But I heard a crashing noise and thought perhaps you were in need of assistance," the earl explained, although he saw now that none of the ladies needed help, save perhaps the younger one who seemed in danger of catching flies unless she closed her mouth.

The countess recovered first.

"Indeed, my lord, how kind of you. My niece has recovered from her momentary dizziness, however. Shall we adjourn to the morning room?" said Lady Hereford, now firmly in charge.

After the briefest of pauses she added serenely: "Barton, have my daughter join us."

Lindenwood's morning room was hung in silk damask of palest lemon that precisely captured the sunlight as it streamed in through large windows overlooking a gently sloping lawn. The greensward was surrounded by an expanse of carefully planted rows of pines, cedars, and Scotch firs that shaded the vista in summer and defended it from cold sea winds in winter.

It was one of Juliana's favorite rooms, the ceiling being festooned with pateras and rosettes that gave it the appearance of one of Cook's frosted confections. She often came here to write her meditations and enjoy the view. As she surveyed their visitor, however, she was not at all at ease.

Lord Pembroke was positioned comfortably but carefully on the smallish divan, as if aware that it was not intended to reliably support such as he. The ample daylight allowed Juliana her first real scrutiny of the earl, and she could not deny that the result was impressive.

He looked to be about thirty years of age. Juliana saw that his bottle green superfine coat fit his massive shoulders to perfection, and his buff doeskin pantaloons clung snugly to his muscled limbs. His muslin cravat was tied in a simple but elegant country style, and his finely polished top boots were handsomely set off by the flowering Savonnerie carpet, itself a work of art in shades of wheat and ivory.

Juliana was irritated to find herself fidgeting in her chair like some schoolgirl as she watched the sunlight bestow highlights on the earl's tousled raven hair. Drat the man, she thought as her frown deepened. She fought a rising sense of panic, knowing that her anxiety could only call her to his attention, something to be avoided at all costs.

Lady Hereford, perching regally on a peacock blue chair, also frowned as she watched Juliana, still in her cap and glasses and looking decidedly ill at ease. When would the girl learn to take an interest in her appearance? Well, that was not her concern at the moment, for the countess had her eye on another fish altogether in the person of her daughter, Lady Sarah.

She could not fault her daughter's appearance. Indeed, Sarah was delightfully adorned in a morning dress of Pomona green with a square-cut neckline outlined with a yellow riband. The color was perhaps a bit strong for a lady just turning seventeen, but Lady Hereford did not want her only offspring to look like any insipid miss.

Thus, the countess was quite pleased that Sarah had joined them with a sparkle in her brown eyes and a smile on her face. Lady Hereford was certain the earl would be captivated. She would no doubt have been greatly alarmed to know that her daughter's smile was the result of a highly improper missive she had but moments ago received from a certain squire's son.

"Lord Pembroke, we are delighted—simply delighted!— to know that you are to be our neighbor this summer," Lady Hereford gushed. "How nice to have you in residence at dear Lucinda's family home."

"You are too kind, my lady. Indeed, I fear there is much work to be done on the estate as it has been sadly neglected for years," the earl replied. "Seagate has only recently passed into my hands, and I intend to bring it up to snuff. Indeed, I have fond memories of several summers passed here during my youth, before I grew up to prefer Greek philosophers and the stuffy halls of Oxford."

It was then that Juliana bestirred herself.

"Surely it is odd that we did not see you during that time, my lord, for the estate does march with ours, you know. To be sure, I do not remember you at all," she said, intending to sound all that was polite but involuntarily biting off her words with a rudeness that surprised even her.

"Juliana!" gasped her aunt reprovingly. She turned to the earl and said, "My niece often traveled with her parents, my brother and his wife, when she was young. I am certain she would perforce have been from home when you were in residence."

"Indeed, as I am older than Lady Juliana, there is no reason why she should remember me," Nicholas said genially, privately wondering about the claws on this tabbycat. "In any event, I was here but a few summers and remember little about the country myself."

Lady Hereford brightened. "Just so with my daughter Sarah. We have been in residence the merest time, so she is not yet familiar with the area. To that point, we are most eager to meet more of our neighbors."

Before she could launch into a description of her plans for the ball, Sarah spoke up.

"Oh, yes, Mama!" she said. "For you know there is a fair within the fortnight at Pevensey. I am longing to go! Mrs. Campbell is expected to perform! *The Times* greatly praised her performance in *Measure for Measure* in Bath and said her Isabel was excellently animated and correct. We will see everyone there! Think of the fun!"

"Watching actors and actresses display themselves in front of the entire community is not precisely what I had in mind." Lady Hereford frowned.

"As it happens, my lady, I am also trying to find out more about the village and its, ah, residents. I would be happy to escort the ladies and protect them from any unsavory elements," the earl offered.

Lady Hereford beamed. Perhaps this would serve very well indeed.

"I shall hold you to your promise, my lord," she said. "I am certain that with your protection they will be quite safe."

"Aunt, I doubt we need Lord Pembroke's protection to visit our own village!" Juliana protested, her relief that he had not given her untoward notice turning into desperation as she sought to stop such an expedition. "I have been attending the Pevensey summer fair most of my life, after all. Surely His Lordship has better ways to occupy his time!"

"Truthfully, I do not," Nicholas interjected. "I was in earnest when I said I would welcome the opportunity to find out more about the village. For you see, I am particularly looking for a young woman."

Seeing their startled expressions, the earl hurriedly continued. "That is, I am seeking her on behalf of a friend, an elderly lady who believes she may be her long-lost granddaughter. They were separated when my friend fled France during the Terror, and she has been seeking her granddaughter these years since. As the girl would have been quite young at the time, it is a difficult task, as you might imagine. But I have reason to believe she may have settled in this area."

"Why, how generous of you, Lord Pembroke, to take an interest in such a tragic case," said Lady Hereford, waving a delicate handkerchief in his direction.

But Juliana could only stare. Her pulse had begun to beat alarmingly, and her temples throbbed. That he was mounting such a search was beyond contemplation!

"That is quite a tale, my lord," she managed to say, unable to banish a note of skepticism from her tone. "Just what does this young woman look like? Perhaps we may be of assistance."

Nicholas studied Lady Juliana, who did not look at all as though she wished to be helpful. Moreover, he was at a loss to explain the lady's displeasure at his presence and her manner that bordered on surliness.

In a less dowdy gown and without those off-putting spectacles and cap, she might be pleasant enough to look at, he mused, if she could but curb that acid tongue. From the look of the unruly auburn curls that refused to be restrained, she might well be more than that. But Nicholas dismissed such thoughts and forced himself to concentrate on the task at hand.

"She looks to be about twenty, with reddish hair. She speaks excellent English. More than that, I'm afraid I cannot say," he replied.

"You have seen her, then," Juliana persisted, her knuckles growing white as her hands clasped the arms of the chair.

"No—that is, I am only guessing, from the lady's description, of how her granddaughter would appear," Nicholas said quickly.

Juliana pushed her spectacles further up the bridge of her nose and nervously barked a laugh. "That description would fit half the female émigrés in England!"

The earl shook his head, wondering how long Lady Juliana would insist on gracing them with her presence.

"You are right, of course," he said with a rueful smile. "Perhaps I will learn more in Pevensey."

Juliana gave a sniff of disbelief, and Nicholas decided the moment had come to take his leave.

As he rose, he added, "I understand the marquess is away at the moment, but when he returns, I would like to meet him at his earliest convenience to discuss some modifications I propose to the fencing between our properties."

"My brother is abroad indefinitely," Juliana said as she too rose with what she hoped was a semblance of dignity. "Any proposals you have can be discussed with me. I have the management of Robert's estate."

If the earl was surprised, he did not show it.

"I look forward, my lady, to our discussions." He bowed, inwardly groaning in dismay.

Juliana remained in the morning room for a long while, attempting to recover her calm self-possession. One thing was certain. She must find a way to miss the summer fair.

3

There was never yet philosopher,
that could endure the tooth-ache patiently.
—SHAKESPEARE, *Much Ado About Nothing*

AS NICHOLAS RODE back to Seagate, he inhaled the misted
air and was filled with a sense of longing, for what precisely
he could not have said. But he knew it had something to do
with his perilous adventure with a certain French spy. He had
been unable to shake the image of that night from his mind,
nay, even his dreams. He was not certain he would recognize
her again, for he never saw her face clearly. But he thought
that in some manner he would be alert to her presence. His
visit to Lindenwood had strengthened his resolve to find his
mystery woman, no matter what the cost.

He laughed as he thought of the taradiddle he had invented
in the marquess's morning room. Long-lost granddaughter,
indeed! The tale would serve nicely as a cover for his search.
That harpy Lady Juliana might even be of assistance since
she was familiar with the area, if he could but overcome her
reluctance.

He further congratulated himself on remembering his
mother's long-neglected childhood home, which would be
an ideal base of operations. Nicholas had in fact been appalled

at its condition when he arrived from London. Restoring the estate would provide an admirable excuse for his Sussex sojourn.

Nicholas was persuaded that the Frenchwoman had some connection to the area. Clearly she had had assistance the night of their arrival in England, perhaps even from the village of Pevensey itself.

Upon reaching land that night, Nicholas and Marie had been met in the darkness by two figures, one of them a short barrel of a man who waited with a horse for her. Nicholas put a hand on her shoulder to stay her leaving, but she silently shook it off and put her finger to his lips. Pulling her cloak around her, she mounted the waiting horse and disappeared into the night followed by the stocky man.

The other figure, whom Nicholas marked as one of James's minions, silently escorted him to an inn an hour's ride away. Exhausted, Nicholas had fallen into a deep sleep, waking late in the day to word from the innkeeper that a carriage awaited to take him to London. Another of James's touches, he surmised.

He had ridden immediately to James's house in Berkeley Square. The two men had been close friends and colleagues at Oxford. While Nicholas had pursued his love of the classics, James had studied history and later won appointment to the Foreign Office. Diplomacy suited James well, for he was at his core a deliberate man imbued with heartfelt dedication to his country.

That was not the image he presented to Society, however. As Nicholas marched into James's study, he saw at once that his friend was playing the dandy to the hilt. His coat of claret kerseymere was unexceptional, but he had let his tailor run wild in fashioning a waistcoat of parrot yellow. His cravat was tied in a complicated style Nicholas had no doubt was James's own creation. It forced his head to remain at a jaunty tilt that would have lent another man a pompous air. James, however, never adopted the unapproachable manner typical of many of his peers, though he was not above using his quizzing glass to deliver a withering setdown where needed.

But that was rare. Most of the time James was relentlessly cheerful, despite the fact that at only thirty-four he walked with a limp. He blamed that on an inconvenient hunting accident. Only a few intimates knew he had sustained his injury during a secret diplomatic mission on the Continent. James was, Nicholas reflected, irritatingly devious.

Nicholas had entered James's study without waiting to be announced. He was as angry as he had ever been, though passionate displays of temper were not in his nature. The earl was not one to seek out conflict, being possessed of a disposition that welcomed congenial congress with his fellow man. And while he was a man of serious pursuits, he rarely took himself too seriously. But at that moment, though he bore his anger silently and gave no immediate evidence of his state, he was a towering fury.

James was happily ensconced at his desk behind a sheaf of papers and greeted his old friend with a smile. As usual, his blond hair was fashionably tousled.

"It is excellent, as always, to see you, Nicholas," James said, his pleasant baritone carrying just the trace of an equally fashionable—and studied—lisp.

As his greeting drew only stony silence, James pulled out his quizzing glass in an amiable and ostentatious inspection of his friend.

"Though I can't say I've seen you looking so out of sorts before. Was your trip not fruitful? Has someone appropriated your latest scholarship? Was your paper not well received? Never say there is a ring of Aristotelian thieves about!"

James folded his hands and smiled expectantly, but

Nicholas's eyes narrowed at his friend's sanguine demeanor. He walked over to the desk and looked down at James from his great height.

"I should call you out," Nicholas said, the quiet sound of his voice arresting his friend's hands as they were in the act of beginning to twiddle their thumbs.

James's smile froze.

"You have played me for a fool and, I suspect, done no better by a hapless French chit," Nicholas said. "I would have expected better from you, James. But as usual you have been dipping deeply into your bag of tricks without regard for those who must pay the consequences."

This time James's smile disappeared, to be replaced by a look more somber than his *tonnish* friends would have imagined. The silence hung heavy around them. Finally James sighed and rose from his desk to seek out a decanter of brandy that rested on the mahogany sideboard. He poured two glasses.

"Sit," he commanded, gesturing to two well-stuffed chairs by the fireplace. Gone was the lisp.

Nicholas warily eased his large frame into a chair as James took the other one and handed him a glass.

"I take it there were, ah, difficulties in delivering my message," James began. "Perhaps you had best start at the beginning, my friend."

"Oh, there were no problems, James. Other than that the courier who gave me your packet was killed, and I found myself stuck in a very unfriendly tavern with only a slip of a barmaid to rescue me from Napoleon's soldiers. Why did you not tell me you were preying on French women desperate enough to betray their emperor? It would have made a much better tale, really, rather than simply commanding me to deliver a parcel on return from my rather prosaic academic exercise."

The words were delivered quietly, without apparent emotion. James said nothing as he studied Nicholas's face, which seemed to be carved in stone.

"What else?"

"Other than riding hell for leather to the sea, crossing the channel in a moth-eaten tub, and spending the night in a fleabitten inn—nothing, I'm afraid."

"And the woman?" James asked.

"Oh, she is safe, I'm sure. Not that you gave that a care. Whoever she is, she was swallowed by the night after we arrived. Quite the woman of mystery," Nicholas responded, studying the rim of his glass as he nonchalantly rubbed away a thumbprint.

James took a drink of his brandy. He sat the glass on the table between them. After a long silence, James spoke.

"It is clear that you do not approve of my methods, my friend. I am sorry you were drawn into such an intrigue. It should have been a routine errand," he said. "Events conspired against us, however."

Nicholas's eyebrows arched as he fixed James with a speaking look. James rose and walked over to refill his own glass. He offered Nicholas the decanter, which the earl accepted.

"Nicholas, I am not at liberty to disclose much about my work. It is not too much to say, however, that we are in an extremely delicate position just now," James said.

"The armistice . . ." Nicholas began.

"Will not last," James interrupted.

He shifted his weight and looked away from the earl.

"The armistice is not in England's interest, for it does not contain the Corsican nor protect our maritime concerns," James said. "Moreover, the Allies are presently in disarray, and Austria is playing a dangerous game of fence-sitting. No, we most certainly do not want this peace."

"If not peace, what then?"

James returned to the chair and said nothing for a time.

Then he leaned over to put a hand on Nicholas's sleeve.

"I trust you implicitly, though I know I have not earned your trust in return. But I must ask that you repeat none of this conversation," James said.

Nicholas nodded his assent but remained silent. James sat back in his chair.

"Our treaty with Sweden has been much debated and not uniformly well received, I'm afraid. But it is essential to our diplomacy," he said.

"You mean war strategy, don't you, James? Let us dispense with your office's polite and meaningless words," Nicholas interrupted, the irritation in his voice betraying, finally, his impatience.

James shrugged. The clock struck the hour then, and he seemed lost in thought. Finally he spoke again, weighing his words carefully.

"It is not yet known that Sweden will formally enter the Allied camp and that we ourselves will join the coalition," he said. "Castlereagh has this month pledged two million pounds to Russia and Prussia to support the war effort."

Nicholas gave a low whistle. James continued in a voice so quiet that Nicholas had to strain for the words, which, when they came, were full of passion:

"We are now irrevocably committed to restoration of the Low Countries, and nothing less than the complete destruction of Napoleon's government and his banishment from continental affairs."

Nicholas felt an involuntary ripple down his spine.

"So you see," James went on, "we face strategic questions that can only be addressed by knowing as much as possible about Napoleon's plans."

"My trip to Paris . . ." Nicholas said.

"Was most convenient," James finished. "We needed to get some information out, but our man was being watched. With your safe passage you were an ideal messenger. Oh, we knew you would most likely be searched at Calais, which is why you were told to digress south a bit. As it developed, it was not safe for you to return to Calais for the crossing. You had an able rescuer, I am sure."

Nicholas looked askance at James, wondering if his friend had intended the last remark as a joke. But James's face wore no smile. Rather, he seemed at that moment to have aged a decade. Nicholas swirled the contents of his glass. He knew James had told him more than he ought. He also knew he would get little else, friendship or no. But there was an unspoken question between them.

James sensed it. He rose to poke at the fire and then leaned on the mantel to study his friend with apparent nonchalance.

"It is the woman, is it not?" he asked softly.

Nicholas fixed his piercing blue eyes on the baronet, whose casual pose was belied by a note of anxiety in his voice. He wondered not for the first time about James's relationship to the woman.

"Who is she, James? More to the point, where is she? And why have you embroiled her in your intrigues? Surely she is but a girl!" Nicholas said.

James shook his head, and Nicholas again was struck by an uncharacteristic tension in his friend.

"Nicholas, I cannot help you there. You must forget about her and let us say no more of it," James entreated.

The earl rose and bowed.

"As usual, James, your brandy was excellent. I cannot say the same, however, for your advice," he said.

As he made his way to the door, Nicholas turned.

"Nothing will go beyond these walls, James. You have my word on that," Nicholas said, looking down at his lapel and brushing away a speck of lint.

Abruptly the earl's head came up, his eyes fixing James with a piercing and direct stare.

"But I find," Nicholas continued with a grim smile, "that it is the woman, after all."

Placing his hand on the door pull, Nicholas gave a bitter laugh.

"I shall not call you out—this time."

James watched his friend leave with a frown. He knew Nicholas would pursue the matter with all of the dogged determination he brought to ferreting out arcane Greek knowledge. James returned to his desk and, after a moment, decided to put pen to paper.

4

I see, lady, the gentleman is not
in your books.
No, and he were, I would burn my study.
—SHAKESPEARE, *Much Ado About Nothing*

JULIANA EYED THE clouds out the window in her aunt's chamber with dismay. It was not a day for a fair. If the weather held this morning, of a certain they would be drenched by afternoon.

"Aunt, I cannot think it is aught but folly to embark on this excursion. You have but to look at the sky," Juliana said, though she had no real expectation that her aunt would relent in her determination for this expedition. But she pressed on.

"Moreover, I have told you I have no wish to expand upon my acquaintance with Lord Pembroke or to help him on his havey-cavey search for some long-lost French female."

Lady Hereford frowned.

"Quit pacing, Juliana! It is not like you, my girl, to put yourself above the wishes of others. You must know I have hopes that Sarah can fix the earl's interest. And if he wishes to aid an elderly lady's quest for her granddaughter, it can only but add to my estimation of his character. You must see, moreover, that your presence is required today. Sarah must not go unchaperoned."

Juliana sighed in resignation and forbore to point out that Lady Hereford could very well act as chaperon herself. Her aunt, however, had already declared that she simply must keep to her room this morning to write to her Edward. At all events, she vowed, she could never keep up with the young people.

So it was that the earl was greeted by a delightful Lady Sarah, adorned in the sunniest of *jonquille* gowns with a matching parasol, and by a glum Lady Juliana, whose only concession to the trip had been to remove her spectacles and don a drab manila brown traveling dress. Her hair was tucked under a matching bonnet.

She could not help but consider that Pembroke cut a dashing figure in his claret waistcoat and buff inexpressibles topped by a flawlessly tailored cutaway in dark blue. Standing beside him as he helped her into his carriage, Juliana was struck anew by his imposing height and surprised by the open, friendly face that was even now smiling down at her.

"You are looking well, Lady Juliana," Nicholas said, and meant it. Although he did not care for her dowdy gown, without her spectacles and cap she seemed less the dour spinster and more the self-assured lady of the manor. Perhaps it would not be an overly unpleasant task to win her good graces.

"You are too kind, my lord," she replied. She noted he had anticipated inclement weather by bringing a closed carriage. "But do you not think, sir, we risk the wrath of the gods by venturing out in such threatening weather?"

Nicholas smiled as he positioned himself next to her in the carriage and signaled the coachman to drive on.

"The gods, like the poet, prefer probable impossibilities to improbable possibilities," he replied.

Sarah looked up in confusion, but Juliana smiled in spite of herself.

"Did the Greeks have an answer for everything?" she asked.

"Would that they did, for I have spent much time pursuing the ancients' knowledge of life's mysteries," he said. "But I have had occasion to find that ancient philosophy is no friend in the pursuit of puzzles of more recent origin."

Juliana looked across to Sarah, who sat with her maid Jenny and was not the least interested in erudite conversation. In fact, Juliana had a suspicion Sarah's mind—and heart— were elsewhere.

"And just what new mysteries are you pursuing, my lord?" Juliana asked lightly, unable to prevent herself from staring into Nicholas's smoky eyes.

Nicholas returned her gaze with a warm one of his own. In truth, he found himself struck by the directness of her green eyes, which had been hidden behind the spectacles she had worn on their earlier meeting. They reminded him of another pair of flashing emerald orbs, and Nicholas again felt a pang of longing for his mystery woman. He turned quickly to gaze out the window.

"Why, only those that haunt my dreams, my lady," he answered quietly.

Juliana colored. And knew in an instant that the trip ahead meant disaster.

Pevensey was a modest seaside village whose citizens were not given to frivolous endeavors, owing to their having to spend much of life toiling for the daily catch which— notwithstanding certain of them who pursued free trade on the sly—constituted their livelihood. A casual observer would have found little here to enchant. Indeed, outsiders were often treated with all the warmth reserved for the king's taxmen. They were a suspicious lot, these fishermen. Life had ever been harsh and ever would be thus. That lesson, above all, had been learned by even the most callow stripling.

But once a year, in the teeth of summer, the village took its merry pleasure in the form of Summer Fair. From nearby Hailsham, and indeed from around Sussex, came gentlemen and gentleladies to sample the wares of the village cooks and craftsmen, Pevensey being noted for its pickled fish and superb basketry. Troupes from London often made Pevensey part of their circuit during the summer. The village was also not so far from Brighton as to make it an inconvenient side jaunt for any of those fashionables who might take it into their heads to wander beyond the prince's immediate circle.

So it was that the ladies Juliana and Sarah, accompanied by Lord Pembroke, found themselves swept up in the festivities surrounding the performance of *Much Ado About Nothing* by Mrs. Campbell's company. Mrs. Campbell herself was to play the tart-tongued Beatrice, to Sarah's delight. She had hoped that Mrs. Campbell's particular friend, Mr. Charles Kemble, might play the role of Benedick, as he had on many noted occasions, but in this at least she was disappointed.

There being no formal theater in Pevensey, the actors used a barn adjacent to the Fish and Kettle, the village inn. It was a mean structure weathered by the gales of many a December and creaking with the age of many decades. On this day, however, it might have been Covent Garden. A green cloth in tatters had been suspended from the ceiling to serve as a curtain. Paper screens had been erected at the right and left of the stage area to create wings. A hoop perforated with nails from which burned tallow candles had been suspended from the ceiling to resemble a chandelier. Spare benches from the inn formed boxes for the patrons.

The meagerness of the setting had not diminished the production's appeal. For there were more than threescore in the audience when the trio from Lindenwood slipped into the back of the crowded barn, electing to stand rather than to maneuver among the seated patrons for the few remaining seats.

"Oh, but this is wonderful above all things!" trilled Sarah, clapping her hands as the curtain made its wobbly rise on the midday performance.

Nicholas smiled at the young lady's pleasure.

"Indeed, it is one of my favorite plays as well," he said. "For though it be comedy, I have always found much wisdom there."

Juliana's eyebrows rose as she turned to the earl.

"I do not believe your Greeks—Aristotle, for one—approved of comedy," she said.

Nicholas allowed himself a moment of surprise, for his acquaintances did not include fashionable ladies familiar with Aristotle.

"I believe scholars would say not that he found it inferior, ma'am, but that he saw it as having a different purpose than tragedy, which he believed was more ennobling," he said.

"Only philosophers see tragedy as noble," Juliana said with a trace of bitterness.

"Or playwrights," Nicholas rejoined with a smile.

The two studied each other for a moment, each knowing a reluctant appreciation for the other's mind. It was Juliana who broke the silence.

"Nevertheless, did not your Greek see the purpose of comedy as one of demonstrating inferior—nay, even ugly—character traits?" she persisted.

"You have the right of it, of course, but it is much as the comedic mask—ugly and distorted, but not evil," Nicholas explained. "Aristotle appreciated comedy as an imitation of persons inferior, but it does not follow that he saw the art itself as inferior. Indeed, he was ever appreciative of its skill. Look, for example, at the masterly fashion in which Shakespeare uses comedy to show us how false appearances can mask true love."

Nicholas stopped himself then, wondering if he was prat-
tling to excess, as he was in danger of doing whenever he
spoke of his beloved Aristotle. But Juliana seemed to ponder
his words carefully. She said nothing and turned her attention
to the play. She was soon caught up in the sharp barbs of
Benedick and Beatrice, and Claudio's mistaken belief that
his love Hero was untrue.

The actor playing Balthasar had advanced to center stage
and was beginning his speech.

"Sigh no more, ladies, sigh no more. Men were deceivers
ever; one foot in sea, and one on shore; to one thing constant
never . . ."

Sarah frowned and turned to Juliana.

"Why surely 'tis an outrage! I am sure men are not deceivers. Indeed," she added dreamily, "I know there are those
whose constancy is a badge of honor."

Juliana shot a concerned glance at her young cousin, and
it was intercepted by Nicholas.

"Well, but besides Don John's trickery, you must admit
that Claudio is not constant in his love. He is too ready to
believe the worst of Hero," he said.

" 'Tis but a play, nevertheless," Sarah said. "And at all
events, I do not believe that either men or women must needs
be deceivers in love. What say you, Juliana?"

"I am sure your knowledge of such matters is superior to
mine, cousin," Juliana replied. "I, of course, do not go out
in Society as you do, nor follow the romantic foibles that so
preoccupy your set."

Sarah threw up her hands in mock disgust.

"You did not answer the question, Juli." She pouted. "I
do think Beatrice would have done better than that."

"She has the right of it, you know," Nicholas said with a
smile. "What think you, Lady Juliana, about women's incli-
nations respecting the art of deception?"

Juliana shifted uncomfortably. She forebore to look directly at the earl, but stared straight ahead and addressed him while seeming to study the actors on stage.

"As to that, I cannot say. But I think it reasonable to assume that women are no more practiced in the art than men. Nor is it in their nature to deceive, any more than it is a man's," she said quietly. "I cannot think, moreover, that it is an enjoyable state when any person must live a life that is a lie."

Nicholas studied her somber face. Despite her sharp tongue, he could sense a maturity of thought and a delicacy of mind that intrigued him. Now that he considered the matter, that atrocious brown traveling gown that was cut with no sense of style appeared to be hiding a rather attractive figure. Nicholas shook his head and smiled to himself. He was not here to study a secluded bluestocking but to find the woman of his dreams. He would have to concentrate better on the task at hand.

"May I prevail upon your kindness, my lady, for an introduction to someone knowledgeable about the area's French population?" Nicholas enquired as he and Juliana left the performance. "Mayhap I can learn something on behalf of my friend."

Juliana's face was suddenly unreadable. Inwardly, she felt herself quake in trepidation. Mentally, she gave herself a shake. She was no fearful green girl, after all! She would show herself a match for this persistent and disturbing earl.

"You will no doubt wish to meet the mayor, who is also the constable and smithy," she said briskly. "I shall take you to him."

The two walked together past booths on the tiny village green, Lady Sarah having begged permission to meet the Misses Harrington at the puppet booth. Juliana led the earl to a gaunt man whose face was a perpetual sea of deep wrinkles.

Jonathan Greeley had seen sixty summers, the last twenty of them as mayor and constable of the village where he had been born. There was little that escaped his notice, and it was assumed, moreover, that he was not a little acquainted with the midnight goings-on in the isolated harbors that ringed the village shores. But Mr. Greeley was a man who held his tongue when the welfare of his village was at stake. For though he did not hold with crime, he could not view his lifelong friends as criminals. Smuggling was a nasty name for what men did to survive, and so Jonathan Greeley was not a man predisposed to talk overmuch to outsiders.

Mr. Greeley gave his lordship a prolonged stare and folded his arms on his thin chest.

"How may I help you, my lord?" he asked with a smile that did not quite reach his eyes.

"I am looking for a French émigré on behalf of an elderly lady who believes she may be her long-lost granddaughter," Nicholas explained. "I was hoping you or someone else in Pevensey could assist me."

Jonathan Greeley rocked back on his heels, favoring this oversized lord with a bland look, for it was well-known that free traders plied their craft with the aid of many an enterprising and often desperate Frenchie. He gave Juliana a speaking glance before turning again to the earl.

"I expect Miss Juliana knows the folks around Pevensey as well as anyone," he said.

There was an awkward moment in which no one spoke. Nicholas frowned in consternation. Clearly the man did not intend to be forthcoming, and Lady Juliana seemed nearly as reluctant to help him as this character.

"I am prepared to ask about, if you have no objections," Nicholas persisted.

One of Mr. Greeley's eyebrows rose slightly as he pondered the consequences of the earl conducting his own investigation. He figured his lordship was not above offering good blunt for a few tidbits. No doubt that would loosen a few tongues. Mr. Greeley coughed. He would let Lady Juliana have the problem of this nosy earl.

"As to that, happens that Nanny Duville be the most knowledgeable French lady around. She knows most everyone, French or no," Mr. Greeley said. "Miss Juliana can supply her direction. If Your Lordship will excuse me, I need to be on my rounds. So many strangers in town, you know."

Mr. Greeley bowed himself away, not before catching Juliana's thunderous look. Nicholas turned to her, anger flashing in his own eyes. When he spoke, his voice was quiet. His words, delivered with a politeness reserved for the drawing room, were, however, laden with accusation.

"Well, ma'am. May I know more about this Nanny Duville? I cannot recall that you mentioned her to me earlier. Perhaps I have only imagined your reluctance on this score. Or is there a conspiracy of silence on this subject?"

Juliana flushed.

"There is no conspiracy, my lord, I assure you," she said with a haughty elevation of her brow. "I am sure it merely escaped my attention."

Nicholas allowed the skepticism to show on his face.

"Well then, just who is the eminently forgettable Mrs. Duville?" he demanded.

There was silence as Juliana pondered the question, knowing the answer would invite his ridicule, yet reluctant to open any corner of her life for inspection. Still, to plead ignorance would only fuel his questions.

"My former nanny," she said.

Nicholas greeted this news with an incredulous snort.

"Ah, yes, one never remembers one's nanny, does one?" he said. "Such an insignificant personage, to be sure."

Juliana knew she had provoked his anger. Nevertheless she found her own growing. Her pace quickened as they

retraced their steps. By the time she had reached the other
side of the green, she was livid. She rounded on the earl, her
eyes flashing.

"You, sir, have no business being angry. In truth, you have
no business here at all. I do not know what is behind your
trumped-up tale of a missing Frenchwoman, but I would
wager it has nothing to do with any noble attempt on your
part to reunite a lady and her granddaughter. As to that,
I doubt there is such a lady! And I cannot imagine what
entitles you to come here like some Bow Street runner
raising questions about matters that do not concern you
at all!"

Juliana paused for breath. Nicholas was staring at her,
open-mouthed. The drab spinster had vanished. In her stead
was some other woman, a woman whose entire body trembled, suffused with the anger that sparkled in her eyes. As
outraged as she was, Juliana had never seemed to Nicholas
more alive and vibrant. Her angry gestures had unsettled
her bonnet, which now dipped over one eye. Juliana angrily
jerked it off, sending a profusion of auburn hair cascading
down her shoulders. Abruptly she turned her head, shoved
the bonnet back on, and stalked off in the direction of their
carriage.

She was more shaken than she could believe. This was
not the way to put Lord Pembroke off the scent, she knew.
Dismayed and mystified at how she could have let her temper become her undoing, Juliana fought for control. By the
time she reached Lord Pembroke's carriage, her anger had
dissipated.

Nicholas had followed this whirlwind, his initial irritation
banished by his puzzlement over her reaction. Lady Juliana's
anger had seemed out of proportion to his inquisitiveness.
Clearly she did not like him. As to why that should concern
him he did not know, for he had no interest in such a prickly
miss in any event.

He found her at his carriage, her back rigid.

"Lady Juliana, I must apologize for causing you any distress. Truly, it was not my intent," Nicholas began. Juliana turned, and Nicholas saw she was once again the impassive spinster.

She inclined her head to him.

"I am certain not, Lord Pembroke. It was I who spoke precipitously. May we forget the matter and cry friends?" she responded, but there was no answering gleam of friendship in her eye. The stiff smile she brought to her lips had, instead, the opposite effect of giving them a derisive curl.

"To be sure, my lady." Nicholas bowed. "Perhaps we should be returning home. I do not care for the look of that sky."

Juliana glanced skyward and saw indeed that it had darkened ominously. She knew that the afternoon already was well advanced.

"I must retrieve Sarah," she said.

Nicholas's coachman, who was standing a respectable distance from the pair, cleared his throat.

"Begging your pardon, Your Lordship, but the young lady has already gone," he said.

"What?" Juliana cried.

" 'Tis what her maid said, my lady. Said the young lady was being taken home by a Mr. Courtney. Jenny was to go along to make it proper and all," the coachman said.

"Oh, drat and bother!" Juliana said. "Aunt Emmaline will have my head for this!"

A roll of thunder startled them both, and several large drops pelted the ground around them.

"I am afraid we must start back," Nicholas said. "This Courtney is known to her?"

"He's Nathaniel, the squire's son. I am afraid I have been a ninny. I suspect Sarah had no rendezvous with the Harrington girls, after all," Juliana said, shaking her head.

Nicholas put a hand under her elbow to direct her to the carriage.

"Your cousin surely will be safe, ma'am. For the nonce, we would do well to secure our own fate."

Juliana sank gratefully into the cushions of Lord Pembroke's well-sprung carriage. This day had been a trial, and she would be relieved when it was over. She glanced over at the earl, who was looking out the window at the giant drops now pummeling the coach. It was then that Juliana realized with chagrin that while Sarah had had the foresight to observe the proprieties by taking Jenny with her, she and the earl were now left completely alone. And in a closed carriage, no less! Her aunt would be apoplectic.

Thus, both Nicholas and Juliana had reason to hope for a speedy and uneventful trip back, as neither wished to prolong the time spent in the other's company. And so it was that neither of them noticed the figure who observed their carriage's departure with a satisfied smirk on his face.

5

There was never counterfeit of passion,
came so near the life of passion as she
discovers it.
—SHAKESPEARE, *Much Ado About Nothing*

JULIANA WAS GRATEFUL that the return trip would not be
a long one, as Pevensey was but a short distance from
Lindenwood. In this, however, she was badly mistaken.

Before they were fairly under way, the sky opened in a
rare fury. Thunder crashed around the carriage as lightning
illuminated what was left of the day. Indeed, it had grown so
dark that it seemed to be nightfall, although Juliana supposed
it was only just past tea time.

The coachman was having difficulty controlling the
horses, judging from the erratic manner in which their
coach was traveling. Lord Pembroke seemed unaccountably
preoccupied with his own thoughts. No doubt it was his
scholar's ability to shut out distractions, but Juliana doubted
whether this tempest could be so easily dismissed. After the
coach jostled them into each other for the third time, the earl
roused himself.

"Devilish storm!" he said after a red-faced Juliana was
propelled into his chest, her bonnet obstructing his vision
and the ribands tickling his nose.

"My lord, I believe we must needs pull over and wait this out. It is folly to push the horses—" Juliana began, only to have her sentence cut off by a horrifying crack that portended that worst of calamities, a broken axle.

For a moment the coach careened drunkenly as the coachman tried to keep it upright, but it was a futile effort. The carriage turned over abruptly, skidded on its side, and came to rest in a ditch. There was an eerie moment of silence and then chaos.

Juliana found herself sprawled on top of the earl, who was crumpled in a heap on the side of the carriage that lay on the ground. His eyes were closed, and he was not moving, but she saw that he was breathing at least.

Her heart sickened as she heard almost human-sounding screams from the horses outside. She moved her limbs gingerly and found that she was amazingly unhurt. After a quick search of the earl's carriage, she located a pistol. Crawling out of the carriage window, she braced herself for what awaited.

The horses were struggling hysterically to right themselves, and Juliana saw with horror that the leader had not only broken a leg but also had partially pinned the coachman. Quickly she walked over to the shrieking animal, put the pistol to his head, and fired.

Nicholas came to with a dim realization that he was in a deuced awkward position and that something hurt like hell. He shook the cobwebs from his head and began to assess his wounds. There seemed to be a good deal of blood coming from his forehead and more from his leg. Then he heard the shot.

"The devil!" he said, and with all the strength he could muster pulled himself out of the carriage. What he saw when finally he stood on solid ground shocked him beyond words.

Pelted by the rain and dodging flailing hooves, Lady Juliana was trying to unhitch the struggling team. And damned near succeeding, Nicholas saw. His coachman was pulling himself from under one motionless animal.

"Let them be, you little fool, else you will be killed!" Nicholas shouted at Juliana, but his voice did not carry above the storm.

He tried to walk and discovered his left leg would not obey, but he found he could manage a hop and skip of sorts by relying on his sound right foot. He made his way to Juliana.

"Let them be!" he shouted again, and grasped her by the shoulders.

A crack of thunder drowned out her cry of victory as the harness came free. The horses found their feet, but with renewed panic, as the earth reverberated with another great boom.

"Their heads! Grab their heads!" came Juliana's shouted plea as the off-leader reared and lashed out.

Nicholas shook his head, trying to clear the fog that had sunk ever deeper in his brain since the accident. He knew that somehow they had managed to reach a barn. He had a dim memory of Lady Juliana holding and calming the horses in a way that he would not have thought possible. He vaguely remembered helping her. He saw that all three animals were now standing placidly in a corner of the barn nosing in the hay.

He remembered leaning on Lady Juliana and John Coachman as they trudged what seemed a great distance in the rain, although it probably was no more than a few hundred yards. He saw that his left trouser leg had been cut away and bound with what appeared to be a piece of petticoat.

"Begging your pardon, ma'am, but as the storm's let up a bit, I'll be going for help," the coachman was saying.

"Nonsense, John," he heard a brisk voice respond. "You

took quite a blow. That arm is practically useless. There is no need for you to go running around the countryside tonight in this. Better you should rest till the morrow."

"But, my lady, His Lordship be needing a doctor, and you and he be in a bad loaf here, if you don't mind my sayin'," the coachman replied, rubbing one arm with a grimace.

Nicholas sat up then and touched his bandaged forehead.

"I assume I am allowed to offer counsel in this strategy session?" he said with what he hoped was a tone of authority as he groggily attempted to rise from the straw.

Juliana and the coachman rushed to him.

"Lord Pembroke, you must not get up just yet. Your injuries . . ." Juliana cautioned.

"Nonsense!" he barked, lifting himself to his feet.

Then he promptly fainted.

Utterly exhausted, Juliana leaned against a bale of hay, her eyes half-closed and her labored breathing the only sound in the darkness besides occasional snorts from the horses. She had just checked the bandage on Lord Pembroke's head and was relieved to see the bleeding showed no signs of resuming.

What a stubborn man, she thought, staring down at the earl as he slept in the straw. In repose he looked harmless enough, his craggy face peaceful and those penetrating eyes closed for the moment. Inexplicably Juliana felt tears come to her own eyes as she fingered the letter in her pocket. She knew this sleeping giant meant danger, and for once in her life she did not know whether she could face it down. Lord Pembroke was clearly not a man to let a puzzle rest until he had poked at it and studied it and exposed it to his scholar's eye.

If only Robert were here, she thought. But, she thought with a wry smile, her brother was facing far greater danger than she.

Juliana drew a deep breath. She hoped John Coachman would make Lindenwood. She was so tired. She wanted so desperately to rest. Her eyelids fluttered, then were still.

It was the kiss that awakened her. Feather-light, it caressed her lips with infinite tenderness, bringing Juliana to the edge of wakefulness with a smile on her lips. She felt herself being folded into strong arms and a warm, firm body and knew a moment of contentment before she drew a gasp of alarm and opened her eyes. She saw that her amorous assailant was Lord Pembroke and that she was lying next to him in the straw. One look at his face told her he was dreaming or feverish, insensible of his actions. She opened her mouth to enlighten him and knew instantly that was a mistake, for his mouth reacted to the movement of hers as fire to a bed of dry leaves.

He kissed her with such passion that his lips became a weapon, commanding her to respond. In a flash his arms tightened around her as he covered her mouth and probed it with his tongue. Juliana was breathless. Putting her hands to his chest, she tried to wriggle free. The earl promptly rolled onto her, pinning her hopelessly. His hands began to rove over her body, and Juliana found herself fighting back waves of pleasure as he caressed her breast.

"My lord, Lord Pembroke . . ." Juliana pleaded, but that was all she could manage.

He put one hand under her hips and lifted them to his. She felt her treacherous body arching into his. And knew she was well and truly lost.

He had finally found her, running her to ground in some godforsaken barn where she was applying a bandage to the wounded leg of a big bay. Her hair was down, and it lay around her shoulders like a reddish halo as she worked over the animal, who bore her ministrations with equanimity. He watched silently until he could wait no longer. He placed his hands on her shoulders, and she turned.

She rose to embrace him, her green eyes flashing passion and promise. Oddly, he could not make out her face. He folded her into his arms, then bore her down onto the hay. He kissed her mouth, gently at first. When she opened her lips to his, he could no longer control himself. He covered her face with kisses, imprisoning her in his arms. She wriggled against him seductively, and he rolled over and pinioned her with his body. He heard her voice, as if from afar. As he lifted her hips to his, she arched into him, and he groaned. Strangely, there was a pain in his leg. His hand reached up to caress her hair. Now at last he would see her face. He opened his eyes.

"Juliana!" came Lady Hereford's hysterical shriek from the barn doorway.

Nicholas blinked as he looked down into the ashen face of Lady Juliana Westlake.

6

I hope you have no intent to turn husband,
have you?
—SHAKESPEARE, *Much Ado About Nothing*

"SIRRAH, UNHAND MY niece!" the countess commanded, sweeping into the barn with John Coachman, a groom, and a maid at her heels. The others halted uncertainly at the threshold. Light streamed in the doorway, the gentle glow of a day not far advanced.

Juliana closed her eyes in mortification, then opened them quickly when the earl did not bestir himself. She saw that he was still looking down at her with a dazed expression.

"My lord, I cannot move," she whispered fiercely.

Nicholas blinked, focusing finally on her face, and his eyes widened in shock. He shifted his body off hers and immediately gave a curse of pain.

"It is your leg, my lord. Please do not move, and I will see to it," Juliana said briskly, trying to recover her equanimity as she hurriedly sat up and brushed straw from her dress.

"You will do no such thing!" Lady Hereford pronounced. "This scapegallows deserves no ministration from us, miss, after dishonoring you!"

"Aunt, he did not dishonor me," Juliana snapped, although she blushed furiously as she checked the earl's bandage.

51

"Lord Pembroke was merely dreaming, doubtless deliriously, owing to his injuries."

Lady Hereford shook her head and clasped her hands to her breast.

"Pish! And to think I had him picked out for Sarah, too! Thanks to the fates, I discovered his true character. It would not do to have my own daughter shackled to this . . . rake!

"Though I suppose," she said after a pause, "that you must needs marry him now."

It was that pronouncement that forced Nicholas to give up all hope that he was in the middle of a harmless nightmare. He sat up and looked at Juliana, whose hands trembled as she attempted to bind his wound. She did not return his gaze.

Lady Hereford was poised with a parasol of aubergine, a color that in the earl's opinion should be banned from the morning hours. She wielded the instrument as if she thought she would need to use it at any moment to save Juliana from the blackguard.

"Lady Juliana, Lady Hereford, I can only express my deepest apologies for this dilemma. I assure you I have the highest respect for Lady Juliana and, had I been sensible of my actions, would never have placed her in such a position," Nicholas said.

He reached his hand to Juliana's chin and gently raised it so that she was forced to look at his face.

"Will you do me the very great honor, Lady Juliana, of becoming my wife?" he asked her.

Juliana gave a sharp intake of breath and a cry of dismay.

"No!" she cried. "My lord, that is not necessary!"

She scrambled to her feet to face Lady Hereford.

"Aunt, you mistake the situation. Lord Pembroke has been barely conscious since our unfortunate accident last evening. He has done nothing to compromise me, and there is not the least necessity of even discussing something so preposterous as marriage!"

Her aunt dismissed her protestations with a wave of her hand.

"As if spending the night in this horror of a barn with only horses as chaperons were not scandalous enough, you would have me believe that the little scene I just witnessed was innocent? It won't wash, Juliana!"

Agitated, Lady Hereford began to pace unconsciously, ignoring the animals' interested snorts.

"It is the outside of enough! Your brother will hold me responsible for this muddle, and I do not know what Edward will say!" she said, clasping her hands in front of her.

"There is not the slightest need, Aunt, for anyone to know anything, so I fail to see the reason for the fuss," Juliana insisted, but her aunt cut her off.

"Now, missy, you see the servants at the door. Just how long do you think this secret will hold? You have been removed from Society too long, methinks, if you do not understand that!"

Juliana blanched, and Nicholas struggled to his feet.

"Indeed, madam, I have every hope that your niece will make me the happiest of men by accepting my proposal," Nicholas said, ignoring the pain coursing through his leg and the panic surging through his whole being. "She will have the protection of my name, and there will be naught said against her."

Juliana turned on him in a wild fury.

"Never! I shall leave the country first!" she cried. "I have no wish to wed, sir, and I refuse to be bound by Society's dictates and your misdirected sense of honor!"

Nicholas put his hand lightly on Juliana's shoulder and tried to smile.

"I know it is not what either of us planned, but I suspect we shall manage well enough. I will not mistreat you, I promise, if that is what concerns you," he said.

"Pah! I have no fear of you," she said. "But neither have I a wish to cede authority over my life to the likes of a husband! It won't do! It just won't do at all!"

"It will indeed do and quite well!" interjected Lady Hereford, striding briskly to Juliana's side and grasping her niece's arm. "Come, we have put on a spectacle for the servants and these confounded horses long enough. We shall return to Lindenwood, send for a doctor, and settle this matter later."

"An eminently sensible suggestion, madam," said Nicholas. He looked at Juliana, intending to give her an encouraging smile.

But her face was utterly devoid of expression.

Mutely Juliana followed her aunt out to the carriage, feeling as if she were trapped in a nightmare that would not end. This could not be happening! Marriage would destroy everything! Of a certain, it would destroy her.

In the end, the marriage was accomplished, though none of the parties approached the matter with unbridled enthusiasm. In a calmer moment, Lady Hereford gave Juliana to understand that, to be sure, she could not be forced to marry against her will. This recent scrape, however, gave eloquent testimony to the necessity of altering her altogether unfettered situation, her aunt insisted. Indeed, it was not fitting for a maiden lady, even one so independent as Juliana, to live in her present fashion. Moreover, Lady Hereford informed her niece, as her brother Robert had by his absence abdicated the responsibility of protecting his sister it was rather incumbent upon Juliana's aunt and uncle to see to the matter. To that end, Lady Hereford remained unmoved by Juliana's insistence that it was unexceptional for her to continue at Lindenwood with only servants in attendance. And so Juliana was given a Hobson's choice, as it were. She would either wed Lord Pembroke or remove with her aunt to Lord and Lady Hereford's country estate for the summer and afterward to London for the Little Season.

Juliana knew herself to be in desperate circumstances, for she could not leave else her work could not continue, and that was crucial to her brother's very survival. Yet she did not see how she could get around her aunt and uncle, short of fleeing the country—a course that likewise would not serve the larger purpose.

She was loath to marry, but having extracted a promise from Lord Pembroke that if they were to wed, they would remain at Seagate for the foreseeable future, she began to think along those lines. It was true, she mused, that clandestine activities would be more difficult with a husband about. On the other hand, married ladies did have somewhat more freedom than spinsters, and perhaps one could avoid having to account for one's every move. And so, at a loss for what course to take, she allowed the existing one to continue, hoping against all evidence otherwise that she would yet discover a way out.

Lady Hereford's husband Edward hied down from London to act in Robert's stead in giving his permission for the match and negotiating the settlement. Robert was, of course, applied to, but since no one knew his whereabouts, there was not much hope of a reply to the letter sent to his last known location, a friend's villa in Florence.

Aunt Emmaline, once she had overcome her initial shock at the situation, set about planning the hurried nuptials with some relish, albeit privately congratulating herself for discovering Lord Pembroke's unfortunate proclivities in time to save Sarah. And as Lady Hereford believed that marriage was the only natural state for her sex, she could not bring herself to feel overly regretful at Juliana's fate.

The bride-to-be was observed enduring the preparations with what can only be described as fierce resignation. Indeed, she appeared to be in a dazed state and often disappeared during the day to go riding on a rapscallion of a horse named Rogue, who could be counted on to give as good as he got. Hours later she would reappear, her complexion much improved from the exercise, but she would retire to her room immediately thereafter and emerge for dinner with unusual pallor.

During the fortnight of preparations, the earl paid daily calls to Lindenwood in a game attempt to reassure Juliana of his resolve to make the most of their rather hasty union.

It cannot be said that he was altogether successful, for when he called, Juliana customarily was away on one of her desperate rides. When the earl joined the family for dinner, he was more often than not confronted by a betrothed without spirit, color, or conversation.

In truth, Nicholas was as reluctantly resigned to the marriage as Juliana, though he sometimes allowed himself to wish that she were not so determined to play the martyr. Occasionally he recalled her spirited conversation and pluck during their Pevensey trip and found himself wondering if there might be some bright spots in their marriage, nay, even some common ground. He found himself curious about the lady's upbringing, as that apparently included wide travel with her parents and a healthy dose of the classics. But those subjects never came up during their few awkward conversations. Indeed, the only matter that appeared to concern his betrothed was obtaining his assurances that they would remain at Seagate for the time being. Her spirit seemed to have vanished, and Nicholas found he rather preferred even the tart-tongued tabbycat to this pallid creature.

Finally Nicholas decided to waylay Juliana before her ride. That these rides usually coincided with his customary hour of calling had not escaped his attention, and this day he arrived early to seek Juliana out. He caught up with her as she was striding vigorously toward the stables where her sour-faced and rotund groom Peters waited as usual.

"Lady Juliana, it would be my very great pleasure to ride out with you today," Nicholas said, only to have Juliana turn and view him with alarm.

"I do not wish to interfere with your daily exercise, but I do feel we must speak privately," he added with a smile that he hoped would allay her reservations.

Juliana looked a silent appeal to Peters, who stood with his customary scowl but otherwise made no move toward her mount. Finally she shook her head. She would not share the pleasure of her ride, but she could think of no excuse to avoid the earl and so allowed him to take her arm.

"Perhaps a stroll, my lord, if you are determined to talk. Though I cannot think what we have to say to each other," she said.

"On that point I believe you are in error, but I will allow you to prove me wrong if you can," Nicholas replied, smiling.

Juliana looked up at him, allowing her eyes to meet the blue-grey ones that were gazing at her with soft understanding. She looked away angrily. She would not suffer his pity.

"How may I serve you, my lord?" she said abruptly.

Nicholas did not answer immediately, but let her lead him through a copse of pine and down a path to a knoll overlooking the sea. It should have been a peaceful walk, as they were warmed by the morning sun and brushed by restful sea breezes. Above them stood Lindenwood, gently sheltered by a grove of trees. Below, lay rocks worn smooth by the comforting rhythm of the sea as it lashed the shore.

But both of them were uneasy. It was Nicholas who finally spoke.

"It pains me, my lady, to be the instrument for forcing marriage on a woman who so keenly treasures her independence and who would never have freely chosen this path," he said.

Juliana allowed her gaze to sweep across the horizon where, somewhere beyond the vast expanse of water, lay France.

"What I would choose is not the issue, my lord, for choices have been made for us both, many times over," she replied. "We can only do what seems necessary. There is no other way."

"Your attitude is understandable, perhaps, but I would hope we can approach this union with something other than resignation," Nicholas said. "I do believe we have more than circumstance in common, and I would that we make our marriage more than one of forced convenience."

He paused, waiting for her response.

Juliana blushed but forced herself to turn and look at him directly. She took a deep breath. Perhaps she could yet induce him to cry off. Juliana knew that happy event would still leave her with the difficult task of defying her aunt. But she suddenly felt overwhelmed by a fear she could not name. Looking into those blue-grey eyes, Juliana knew it had something to do with the way she found herself trembling when he studied her with just such an expression as he wore now. She plunged ahead.

"My lord, as long as we are speaking frankly, let me say that I hope not to be a grave disappointment to you as a wife. But I must tell you that my heart is otherwise engaged."

She saw that her statement had the intended effect. Nicholas looked at his wife-to-be in shock and dismay. Before he could react to this revelation, Juliana went on.

"I have obligations I cannot discuss," she said. "If you will in truth allow me my measure of independence, we will have a tolerable union. If not, I cannot account for the future and fear we will both be the unhappiest of persons."

Juliana walked slightly away from him, willing herself not to tremble. She clasped her arms around herself.

"I shall, of course, endeavor to perform my wifely duties. You need have no concern on that score."

With that, she returned her gaze to the sea.

Nicholas was thunderstruck. Nothing in his past contact with Lady Juliana had prepared him for this. That this strange spinster was wildly in love with someone else was beyond his imaginings. The future seemed bleak all of a sudden. Still, he was more determined than ever not to add to her misery. He walked over to her and put his hands on her shoulders. He felt her shiver.

Juliana turned and saw that his eyes were grave.

"I confess myself somewhat at a loss, my lady, as to your news," Nicholas began haltingly. "I fear I was not prepared to hear that my betrothed was in love with someone else."

Juliana opened her mouth to speak.

"No, pray do not," he said with a wry smile. "I must have my say, you know."

This time it was Nicholas who turned to the horizon for inspiration. When he spoke, his voice had a remote, dreamlike quality.

"I had not thought that I would marry, you see, at this point in my life. Rather, I have been concentrating on . . . other matters," he said. "I do not know, really, what I want in a wife. It has not seemed important until now."

He was silent for a long moment, and Juliana ventured a sideways gaze at his impressive profile. His face, outlined against the sky, bespoke a strength of character as well as that of a more physical nature, she found herself thinking. Mesmerized, she could not tear her eyes away. He continued to stare at the sea, unseeing.

"In truth, I suppose I would like a woman to share my life, my love of learning, and my own particular view of the world. Someone who is as comfortable with me as I am with her," Nicholas said. "Who wants me in her bed as much as I want her."

Juliana felt her face redden, and inexplicably, tears came unbidden.

"Nevertheless, as you stated, we have no choice," he said, looking down at her with a gentle smile. "Whoever is fortunate enough to possess your heart is not presently in a position to take my place, I gather?"

Juliana looked away and gave a barely perceptible shake of her head.

"Then I have a proposition that might make our union more bearable," Nicholas continued.

Nicholas grasped Juliana's hands and drew her to sit with him on a rock. He put one of his hands over hers and with the other gently touched her chin.

"I propose that we do not live together as husband and wife. I have no wish to force myself on you, at all events, as I have tried to make plain," Nicholas said.

Juliana's eyes widened. She heard his words, but she could not credit them.

"If, at the end of the required period, we do not wish to remain married, we will obtain an annulment," he said.

Juliana gasped. "But that would mean three years!"

"I know it is a long time," Nicholas admitted, "but it is not forever. We would both still be young enough to remarry. There is time yet before I must set up my nursery. And there would be no scandal attached to an annulment. I would, of course, make a generous financial settlement on you."

He coughed awkwardly and added, "And during our marriage, you would have all the independence you craved . . . within, ah, the bounds of discretion and honor. That is to say . . . well, I hope I need not speak more plainly." Juliana knew her face was the color of barberry.

"But for an annulment you would have to declare . . . that

is, you would have to make known . . ." she began, but could not make herself continue.

"I must admit a legal declaration of impotence is not overmuch to my liking." The earl laughed. "But it pales beside my distaste of forcing us to continue in a union neither of us desires. I suppose I am a romantic, after all, though you can hardly blame that on the Greeks."

Juliana was unable to speak. She had not been prepared for this man's generosity. Of a sudden, she had her life back again. All would be as before.

Nicholas studied her face, searching for a reaction. Finally her face broke into a tentative smile.

"I accept your proposition, my lord," Juliana said. "Let us cry friends."

And this time there was a tiny glow of friendship in her eyes.

7

Shall I never see a bachelor of threescore
again? Go to, i'faith; an thou wilt needs
thrust thy neck into a yoke, wear the print
of it, and sigh away Sundays.
—SHAKESPEARE, *Much Ado About Nothing*

JULIANA OPENED HER eyes to see that she was surrounded
by blue the color of a sparkling clear sea. It transformed the
walls into a reflection of the sky outside the windows that ran
the height of her chamber. Above her, topping the enormous
carved bed in which she lay, was a huge canopy on which
damask of this self-same hue was fastened. The fabric trailed
down the bedposts, imparting the comforting feeling of being
surrounded by this extraordinary color—as if, she imagined,
one were reclining in an open boat of a quiet afternoon.
Outside the gulls chattered noisily as they went about their
business. Juliana smiled lazily and stretched out her toes.

Abruptly her smile faded, and she sat bolt upright. In a
calmer moment she would have marveled at the memory
lapse that had allowed her, however briefly, to forget that
this beautiful morning was—oh, horror!—that which followed her wedding day. But now she knew only a sense
of rising panic that caused her heart to pound. She was
Lady Pembroke. Juliana shook her head. Had ever a bride

begun a marriage thus? But then, hers was hardly like other marriages.

An image of Lord Pembroke, as he had looked as they said their vows, thrust itself before her. Their wedding had been held in Lindenwood Chapel as it was felt by all parties that, under the circumstances, a quiet affair was everything that was appropriate. Pembroke had obtained a special license, and the matter was quickly accomplished. Juliana overset her aunt by refusing to wear her mother's silver and white gauze confection. Her mother, she reminded Lady Hereford, had made a love match, and Juliana would make no pretext to *that* situation. Instead she wore a plain ivory gown and a single strand of pearls. In her hair, which she pulled back severely at the nape of her neck, she allowed a lone white rose.

Pembroke similarly appeared caught by the somberness of the occasion, impeccably attired as he was in black dresscoat and pantaloons, embroidered silk stockings, laced boots, and a lightly frilled shirt. He wore no jewelry. The simplicity of his garb seemed to Juliana to march with the man; but rather than assure her as to the efficacy of their union, it merely served to unsettle her. For in the perfection of cut and starkness of demeanor, Lord Pembroke's clothes set off to exquisite accomplishment the superior physical attributes of their wearer.

And so Juliana found herself during the ceremony staring resolutely at the toes of her dainty satin pumps so as to avoid those blue-grey eyes that shone like pewter and studied her with piercing attentiveness as Bishop Adams pronounced the words that made them man and wife. At the ceremony's conclusion her new husband bowed to her politely and tucked her arm in his.

The wedding breakfast was a veritable haze, excepting the fulsome toasts that Juliana's uncle Edward had felt it necessary to offer and which succeeded, in their barely veiled allusion to love and lust, in mortifying Juliana beyond all thought. Lord Pembroke had, in unflappable fashion, steered her uncle into other avenues, but Juliana had felt her spirits sink even lower as she began to realize, finally, the magnitude of the step she had taken.

They had decided against a wedding trip or indeed any pretense at acting the rapturous couple. Instead Lord and Lady Pembroke stepped into a coach and four at Lindenwood and traveled less than a quarter hour to Seagate where they quickly disembarked to face a long evening that stretched like a bad play into the night. Conversation was stilted.

"Where is your principal seat, my lord?" Juliana asked at one point, searching desperately for a fruitful topic as they sat before a sumptuous array of silver platters of roast chicken, salmon, lobster, and rabbit fricassee laid out for their private wedding supper.

Nicholas cast her a questioning look.

"I forget we know so little about each other. It is in Essex, my lady, and my ancestors have enjoyed the proximity to town. My father's brother, however, owned an estate in Yorkshire which came into my hands some time ago, and I confess to having retired there once or twice to the peaceful seclusion of my studies," he said. Then he added hesitantly, "We could go there some time if you like."

Juliana gave him a look of alarm, which seemed to momentarily confuse him. Then his brow cleared.

"I have promised we shall remain at Seagate for the nonce, and so we shall," he reassured her. "Though I cannot think to stay here indefinitely, I would have no objection if you wish to make this your home year round."

"And I would have no objection to your absence, my lord. I am certain that your work requires much solitude and diligence that perhaps cannot be accomplished with the distraction of a wife rattling about," Juliana returned politely.

Although there was much more that could have been said

on this topic, neither party seemed eager to pursue it. The meal took on a strained atmosphere, and Juliana prayed only for its end. Finally her husband suggested that as they were both looking rather peaked, an early night might be of benefit. He had escorted her to the door of her new chamber, bowed slightly, and bid her goodnight.

Looking around now at her chamber, which was really quite charming, Juliana sighed. If she were not careful, she would spend her entire married life with a case of the megrims. A breeze blew into the room, bringing with it the fresh air of the sea and cheering her slightly. Juliana resolved to cast off her low spirits. After all, her husband was no more desirous of this marriage than she. Perhaps they could strive for a measure of friendship. The only difficulty, she mused in chagrin, was that she found it difficult to think of Lord Pembroke in those terms.

She knew beyond all doubt that he posed the gravest sort of threat to her. On the one hand, he sought to expose her game, for if he found his "Marie," surely the result would be catastrophic. On the other, he threatened her steely and hard-fought equanimity. She did not precisely know how that happened, but she had observed on the occasions in which she had been in his presence a certain quickening of her pulse, a wetness to her palms, and a tendency to abandon her self-possession and fly up in the boughs.

How could she maintain a friendship with such a man and likewise keep him at arm's distance? She swallowed hard and rang for her abigail. It was time to find out.

Nicholas peered over the rim of his coffee cup to meet the eyes of his new wife. She had clearly taken little pains with her appearance, he saw with resignation, and she was looking at him with a too-bright smile, at least it seemed so to Nicholas, given the circumstance that they were beginning what amounted to a three-year sentence together. It was not that he found his wife repulsive. In fact, he liked her well enough, although she had a tendency toward prickliness he could not fathom or enjoy. He appreciated the ordeal that a forced marriage had thrust upon her and had promised himself to do all in his power to make their union tolerable. But as their marriage was to be in name only, and thus devoid of the spiritual and physical sharing that marked the happy joining of two kindred souls, he was impatient to pursue his own interests. He had no intention of abandoning his search for his mystery woman, and beside that exotic paragon, all others paled.

"Allow me to express my utter delight, my lord, at the chamber you have chosen for me. Truly, it conjures the sea in all its best moments, and I cannot think when I have seen a more beautiful shade of blue. It is joyous perfection itself," Juliana trilled, and though indeed she was delighted with her room, the words sounded even to her a bit florid and unnatural. Still, she was determined to be amiability itself.

She thought he colored slightly. Though she could not know it, she had touched a responsive chord, for Nicholas had especially ordered the outfitting of her chamber, thinking to make his bride as comfortable as possible and choosing a sea theme as that which most recalled her beloved Lindenwood. And as Nicholas was no more immune to compliments than most, he could not help but be flattered by her words, though he loathed excessive flattery.

"You are too kind, my lady. It is my wish to make you welcome at Seagate, although you will see presently that there is yet much work to be done to make it truly habitable. As for your chamber, it pleases me greatly to have been the architect, however superficially, of your happiness," Nicholas replied.

He was not over-pleased, however, at the odd way his words sounded to his ears. His reference to her superficial happiness seemed uncharitable and could not but serve to remind them both of the unusual and unwelcome circumstance of their marriage. He glanced quickly at her in the hope that she had not taken his statement amiss. Unfortunately he saw that Juliana held her cup in midair and appeared to be in the act of gathering her resources for a response.

Juliana forced herself to retain her smile. As she was determined to control her temper, she took a measured sip of the bracing liquid and gave her husband a benign look.

"Indeed, my lord, as to my happiness, I am pleased that you consider yourself responsible for even such a small measure of that quality which falls within your power to influence," she replied in the sweetest of tones.

Nicholas felt his own blood rise. He had intended nothing untoward by his remark and was not pleased at the way Juliana had turned it back on him. Moreover, he did not like the false politeness of this conversation that he suspected masked a wealth of ill will. If this was to be the tenor of their mealtime conversations, Nicholas thought, it would be imperative for his sanity to arrange to eat elsewhere.

"You misunderstand me, my lady. I intended naught amiss," Nicholas said with careful amiability. "It is merely that I am aware that residing at Seagate would not be your preference, absent the unfortunate accident of our Pevensey trip. It is my wish, therefore, to make your life here as pleasant as possible."

"The unfortunate accident, as you are pleased to refer to the catastrophe that necessitated our marriage, would not have occurred had it not been for your ill-time nosing about for a creature who, I am certain, exists only in the misguided mind of him who searches," Juliana responded, her eyes flashing.

"Which search, madam, you were heartily guilty of attempting to obstruct at every turn and indeed displaying a duplicitous bent, if I may be so bold as to suggest it, along with a temper that I see now was not an aberration to your own nature," Nicholas retorted.

The two combatants, for it was necessary at this juncture to abandon all pretext at congenial conversation, glared at each other across the table.

Unaccustomed as he was to heated disputes and uncomfortable with the notion of sparring, even verbally, with the woman who—whatever the circumstance—was indeed his wife, Nicholas dashed his napkin onto the table and pushed back his chair.

"Perhaps, my lady, we can abandon this farce of a breakfast. I myself have more rewarding tasks to pursue, and perhaps, I may suggest, you do also. If you need aught," he said as he rose to his full height and looked disapprovingly down at the top of her auburn head, "you must ask my housekeeper, Mrs. Burling. If it is urgent, you are free to send a message to my study."

He turned and left the dining room, adequately conveying the message that he wished not to see her face again that day, Juliana thought. She clenched her fists in frustration. This was not an auspicious beginning.

It was late afternoon when Nicholas sought her out. Juliana was sitting on the terrace attempting to apply herself to a piece of needlework and battling the fading light. She looked up at the sound of a footfall.

"Am I interrupting?" he said, his face half hidden by the lengthening shadows.

Juliana felt suddenly very small as she looked up at the figure of her husband.

"Nay, but pray sit down, my lord, as my neck is a fair way to developing a strain with the effort of viewing you at such a height," she replied, unable to hide the brittleness in her tone. She nearly jumped from her chair as he quickly closed the gap between them.

"I wanted speech with you, my lady," he began, and then broke off abruptly. He cleared his throat and shifted awkwardly before he spoke again.

"To be precise, I have come to offer an apology for my behavior this morning," he said. "For I cannot like being at fisticuffs with my wife."

Juliana looked into the eyes that searched hers for a response. They were not ungentle, she decided. Indeed, at the moment they looked so earnest and regretful that she had to suppress an instinct that bid her to reach up and caress away the wrinkles of concern that lined his face.

"It is my own tongue, my lord, that I failed to govern. Pray, do not apologize because I have not the discipline to control my temper," she said.

To her alarm, Nicholas took her hand between his two great ones and fixed her with a determined look.

"Nay, for I have admired your spirit and your willingness to speak your mind. You must not feel hesitant on that score. It is a pity that I cannot easily manage such frankness myself," he said.

Juliana looked at him in surprise.

"But you have always been straightforward in your manner with me," she said, tilting her head slightly to peer at him.

Nicholas looked discomfited.

"Indeed, madam, I suppose I have tried to be thus, but I must tell you that it is not in my nature to feel overly comfortable in matters of temper," he said. "I cannot like argument, unless it be of an intellectual bent, and when I find myself in the midst of one, I am like as not to simply leave the premises. It is a somewhat cowardly response, but there it is."

Juliana studied the large form of her husband.

"I do not credit your description, sir," she said charitably, "for it has been my observation in our brief acquaintance that

you have a steadfastly determined nature. I would not confuse cowardice with judicious marshaling of one's resources,
and I suspect that when put to it you are the most direct and
courageous of men."

Nicholas laughed in embarrassment.

"I thank you for that, madam," he said. "Perhaps it is
simply that I am more accustomed to dealing with words, not
people, and am more at ease grappling with the problems of
humanity outlined in books rather than the human problems
sitting across from me at table."

"Am I such a problem then, my lord?" Juliana said, her
eyebrows knitted in concern.

He studied her face as he considered a response.

"I truly do not know how to describe you, madam," he
said ruefully.

The ensuing fortnight was largely passed in dedicated
civility, although both parties seemed to strive for a certain
distance in their social intercourse that gave their moments
together a pervasive uneasiness.

Often Nicholas did not appear at mealtime. His excuses
were perfectly plausible, usually having to do with his finding it necessary to inspect some far-flung aspect of the
estate that kept him out of the house much of the day. But
Juliana thought she knew his absences for what they were—
efforts to avoid her. She judged that Nicholas, despite his
apology, was not pleased to have her in his house and was
perhaps pursuing that approach which he had warned her
was his nature.

In fact, Nicholas was discreetly canvassing nearby villages. He spied several red-haired maidens who seemed from
a distance to resemble the woman he sought, but upon closer
inspection they bore the pudding-faced features of sturdy
village stock and in no way matched the object of his search.
In the evening, Nicholas often retreated to his study with

his brandy, brooding over the day's failures. Invariably his thoughts would turn to the woman who was his wife, and if she suffered by comparison to the lady of his dreams, it was no more than could be expected. Juliana was a strange sort of woman, he mused. Despite her forthright manner of speaking, Nicholas sensed a reticence that he could not explain. Perhaps her thoughts were often with that person to whom she had alluded during their conversation at Lindenwood. He had never questioned her further about the circumstances that had kept her from her true love, and wondered whether her frustrations over that matter accounted for her sharp tongue. He tried to imagine his wife as she might appear if she were reconciled with the one she loved. Would there be a soft look about her eyes, perchance, a glow about her face, a gentle trembling about the mouth? His idle wonderings set his thoughts off in an altogether interesting direction, and he found himself trying to conjure an image of Juliana in a moment of wild abandon. Abruptly he gave a bitter laugh. The image had quickly changed into that of an emerald-eyed French girl. He took a last swallow of brandy. His mind was playing tricks on him. It was time to retire.

Nicholas was unfailingly polite to Juliana, as he had vowed there would be no repeat of the open hostility that had flared during that first breakfast. He never approached his wife, taking refuge in a remoteness which it was his habit to adopt when mulling over an especially troublesome problem. Juliana felt the acuteness of his rejection, though why it should trouble her remained a source of perplexity to her.

And so the days ambled by until one evening Nicholas surprised Juliana by coming to the drawing room after dinner. He had lingered too long over his port, although he was usually far more temperate, and now found himself loath to spend the rest of the evening in his own company wrestling with the unbidden images that relentlessly entered his mind.

Juliana's eyebrows rose when her husband entered the room, as she had grown accustomed to his absences, thinking with some relief that this manner of goings on would at least afford her ample opportunity to manage her own absences without much scrutiny. Moreover, she did not miss the rather flushed appearance her husband presented this night, and so gathered her needlework and made a move to rise.

"My lord, I was just about to retire as I find myself much fatigued," Juliana began, but Nicholas put a hand on her shoulder and gently pushed her back onto the divan.

"Nay, Juliana, I would that you spare me some minutes, as it is early yet and I am eager of company," he said, sitting next to her.

It was the first time he had used her given name. Juliana felt his warm breath uncomfortably near and shifted to adjust her position a few inches farther away.

"My lord, surely there is a wide array of chairs you could choose without intruding yourself thus," Juliana said sharply, making a sweeping gesture around the room, where in truth there were nearly a dozen chairs scattered about, the room being large enough for at least a small assembly.

"A thousand pardons, madam," Nicholas replied, his mouth twisting with sarcasm. "I did not apprehend that I was discommoding you by my presence. And to think we have been married but two weeks. Was ever a bridegroom so fortunate in the affections of his lady?"

Juliana rose in irritation.

"Ours is not a marriage of affection, my lord, as I apparently need to remind you," she retorted. "A fact I would trouble you to respect, as well as my person!"

Nicholas allowed his eyes to roam over Juliana's form, encased as usual in a garment that fit so ill as to convey neither form nor figure.

"As for your person, madam, you need not fear that I will attempt it," he replied. "Indeed, you are so far from enticing me to such a rash proposition that I cannot conceive it.

"Although," he began again, rising and moving to stand close to Juliana, "it would be an interesting experiment to find out if there is aught that could move the ice maiden whom I have been ill-advised enough to wed."

With that, he placed his forefinger on her lips, which were parted slightly in outrage, and encircled the smooth flesh. As she stood paralyzed, he caressed first her upper lip and then its mate. His face bent down to hers, and Juliana felt her breathing grow more rapid. His fingers touched her chin, lifting it slightly for his kiss, which, when it came, startled Juliana by its gentleness. His lips touched hers ever so lightly in a teasing fashion, and she remained immobile as, finally, he pressed his mouth more firmly to hers. She gave an involuntary shiver. Her mouth inadvertently opened to his, and her hands, which had been rigid at her side, began to inch upward and reach out for his waistcoat. Nicholas lifted his face and studied her.

"Perhaps, my dear, your abhorrence of the marital state is not so great as you profess," he said softly. "Or is this, perchance, evidence of that warmth you accorded that nameless worthy who is so fortunate as to possess your heart?"

His voice broke the spell that held Juliana and caused her hands to fly to her mouth in horror. She broke from his embrace and strode violently to the window, turning her back to him in a rigid expression of outraged anger.

"We have an agreement, my lord, or is your word merely a convenience that you take on and off like a favorite pair of boots?" she said, as much disturbed by her acquiescence to his attentions as by the fact of them. Moreover, she found she could not control the quiver in her voice.

To her utter disbelief, Nicholas laughed. She gripped her arms in fury.

"I would hold you to your pledge, sirrah," she began, "or . . ."

"Or what, Juliana?" said a voice softly by her ear.

She whirled to face him, but was startled at his closeness and tried to put up her hands to keep distance between them. Nicholas quickly captured her wrists, imprisoning them, and brought his mouth down on hers with a fierceness that surprised them both. As she felt the bruising impact of his lips, Juliana knew a moment of panic that suddenly gave way to helpless surrender to the wave of sensation that began in the pit of her stomach and traveled down to her toes.

There is no way of knowing how long the moment lasted, as participants in such events are known to lose the senses that enable them to mark time. So it was with Juliana and Nicholas, who, suspended in such a moment, knew only the sensation of flesh on flesh and an urgent desire to pursue the matter further.

Abruptly Nicholas thrust her away and turned his back, which suddenly became immobile as if in silent struggle with some unseen force. Juliana barely prevented herself from falling and took little comfort in the sight of her husband's massive back as it was shown to her in apparent rejection. When he turned back to her, his face was grave.

"I would crave your pardon, my lady," Nicholas said. "You have the right to expect some measure of safety, not to mention respect, in your own home. Indeed, it is so far from my nature to turn violent that I can only claim some mitigation from the quantities of port I consumed this evening and perhaps some preoccupying matters that weigh heavy on my mind. I do humbly beg your forgiveness."

This speech, added to the experience she had just endured, so overwhelmed Juliana that she wanted to burst into tears. Instead she took a deep breath and launched a conciliatory speech of her own.

"Indeed, my lord, pray do not humble yourself on my account, though I am startled and, aye, alarmed to find myself in the presence of such . . . warmth," Juliana said awkwardly, her face flushed.

She walked a few paces and then abruptly turned toward Nicholas.

"Truly the circumstances of this marriage must be a trial to you, sir," she said, speaking rapidly. "But as I know you can have no wish to alter the terms of our union, I suggest that it behooves you to exercise your . . . passions elsewhere."

Then, in a voice devoid of expression, she added, "I assure you I would not take it amiss were you to take a mistress. Indeed, it is the way of our society. Therefore, let us have no more repeats of this scene and agree as sensible persons to do each other no more ill."

Nicholas frowned at Juliana's words. It was not that he did not see the sense of them; rather it was that he could not condone the hypocrisy of such an arrangement, whether widely accepted by the *ton* or no. For Nicholas had not spent a lifetime in study of the philosophers in order to adopt a personal philosophy of frivolous convenience. That his own foibles had not yet led him to confront his intentions in searching for his mystery woman—about whom he thought daily—was perhaps not to be wondered at in one who so little liked to confront matters of the heart. To be sure, if asked, he would have said that his intentions were honorable. And that was the crux of it, for Lord Pembroke thought of himself as an honorable man. That he had behaved otherwise with the woman who was his wife was a matter that now gave him great distress. He knew himself deeply regretful over the emergence of his baser instincts and decided that the only way to avoid inflicting further pain on both of them was to absent himself. Without another word he left the room.

8

One woman is fair, yet I am well; another is
wise, yet I am well; another virtuous, yet I
am well: but till all graces be in one woman,
one woman shall not come in my grace.
—SHAKESPEARE, *Much Ado About Nothing*

AS HAPPENS WITH some of life's unhappiness, the morrow
often dulls the edges of difficulty and erases its dark and
brooding corners. So it was that when Juliana awoke, she
was greeted by the remarkable sight of a yet another sunlit
day and, taking the weather as a good omen, formed a
renewed intent of winning her husband's friendship. In this
she surprised herself, for she had expected to feel nothing
but mortification at the thought of facing Nicholas again.
It was true that a blush stole over her face when she
recalled the warmth of certain moments during the previous
evening. Moreover, she was frankly troubled by the anger
that seemed to flare between them with disturbing regularity;
however, she persuaded herself that if they could but adopt
an air of reasonableness and allow their finer sensibilities
to rule, they might avoid such unpleasantness in the future.
She congratulated herself on proposing that remedy most
likely to prevent repetition of the physical assault she
had endured. If honesty forced her to acknowledge that

it had not been such an unpleasant ordeal as all that (and indeed, her own response had served as eloquent testimony to that point), it also allowed her a sigh of relief that such future occurrences had been forestalled. And so she found she quite looked forward to the day with anticipation.

Juliana frowned, however, as she opened her wardrobe, wishing that the circumstances of her masquerade permitted her to adopt more pleasing attire. It was not that she relished playing the dowd. It was simply that she had always been careful not to attract unnecessary notice and had long accustomed herself to hiding her light under a bushel, so to speak. She tilted her head and surveyed the dismal choice of gowns. Well, no one would take much notice of spinsterish Juliana Westlake, and that is how she wished it. Or did she? Juliana gave herself a mental shake. She was Lady Pembroke now, and for some reason today she had a particular wish to please her husband.

But when she walked down the stairs to discover his whereabouts, she was told by the housekeeper that his lordship had gone to London and would be there some days.

Juliana knew a moment of disappointment but refused to let that dispel her relentless cheerfulness. And so she determined to explore the house.

Even a charitable eye would have judged it wanting, for the structure had suffered mightily from years of neglect and abuse from the sea air. Its rehabilitation had come not a moment too soon, as the house surely would have become unfit for habitation ere many more years passed. Nicholas had ordered those rooms most urgently needed—the dining room, drawing room, and Juliana's chamber—immediately restored. But elsewhere the paint was severely faded and the plaster badly cracked. Marble fireplaces also had cracked, revealing inferior stone beneath. Floors had long since lost their polish, and much of the furniture was in disrepair. In the music room, Chinese hand-painted wallpaper hung in shreds.

On the whole, except for those rooms that had been restored, the house gave off a rather dreary air of decay, Juliana decided. She fervently hoped Nicholas would see to it that the renovation proceeded apace, for it would be difficult to maintain her spirits against such a gloomy backdrop.

Juliana opened a heavy wooden door, expecting it to lead into yet another dilapidated room, and found to her delight that it opened into the small but excellently appointed library that Nicholas used as his study and which gave no evidence of disrepair. Bookshelves ran the length and height of the room, and the walls wore a dark oak paneling that lent the library an air of somberness, happily relieved by enormous windows that welcomed the sunlight and sea air. Juliana was drawn to the massive oak desk on which she spied pages of a manuscript.

Some of the writings she could not make out adequately, as they were in Greek, a language in which her understanding was vastly inferior to that of Latin. A few pages in a bold script, which she assumed was her husband's, caught her eye.

"It is not to be supposed," Nicholas wrote, "that although Aristotle—like Plato—viewed the artist as an imitator of life, he likewise saw the artist's product as invalid. Rather, Aristotle regarded art as the technique which realizes matter's full potential."

Juliana settled into the chair and picked up another page, marveling at his clarity of reason.

"There can be, therefore, 'truth in art' proper to itself, rendered by the artist as he goes about his craft," Nicholas wrote. "Truth thus is not an absolute quality to be fastened with rigidity to some pillar of judgment, but rather open to interpretation and often defined by the observer."

Juliana smiled slightly. And what, she wondered, would her husband think if he knew the truth about her? Would he approve of her particular "interpretation" of truth, or would he feel cheated, betrayed, and otherwise outraged to learn that his wife was in fact a spy? She bent her head and read further.

"The Platonic criticism that poetry 'has the same effect on lust and anger and all those experiences of desire and pleasure and pain,' (that is to say, 'waters them and makes them grow when they ought to starve with drought') poses an interesting question," he wrote. "Aristotle maintains that through the purgation of passion—perhaps through music or art—the spectator undergoes a catharsis that relieves him of the burden of those passions. Does art thus exacerbate passion or ease it? It seems likely, in any event, that there are some individuals whose natures have higher susceptibility to passion's sway . . . "

Juliana put down the papers and determined to read no more. She was not especially comfortable with the notion of passion. If she wondered at her lack of success in controlling her own, at least where Nicholas was involved, she found no convenient answer. She was certain, however, that music or art would not relieve her of that particular burden.

She deemed her exploration fruitful, nevertheless, as it presented an interesting aspect of her husband. He had, it seemed, a rich inner life and a provocative scholar's mind. Under other circumstances, perhaps in a different sort of marriage, she thought almost wistfully, she would have enjoyed sharing some of his thoughts on these and other subjects. She shook her head and rose to leave, but her eye was caught by a small note that lay carelessly on the corner of the desk as if cast there in haste. She bent to retrieve it and then blanched. It contained the direction of Elise Duville.

Nicholas gazed at Juliana's former nanny, a petite Frenchwoman who was staring up at him with a distinct air of distrust. He had easily located her cottage, a small but solid two-story stone affair in excellent condition. The structure was nestled in one of those seaside hills that gave the uninitiated observer approaching from landside the misimpression that the sea lay miles beyond. But upon reaching the crest, the climber was apt to find himself looking two hundred feet down a sheer cliff onto foam-lashed rocks.

"*Vraiment, m'sieur,* I know of no such woman as you describe," Elise Duville insisted for the fifth time.

"And I have reason to believe, madam, that you do," Nicholas repeated calmly.

The two studied each other in silence, one that could have continued until Doomsday had not a thought occurred to Mrs. Duville.

"How does it happen, milord, that you are married to my Juliana and yet you seek another woman? Pray, does your wife know of your intrigue?" That delivered in an accusatory tone, Mrs. Duville leaned back in her chair to hear his response.

Nicholas had the grace to look uneasy and the wit to judge that, despite her impertinence, she would likely tell him nothing if she thought it would harm Juliana. She had merely sniffed dubiously at his tale of an elderly French émigré looking for her long-lost granddaughter.

Finally he simply fixed her with a bland gaze and informed her, with a stubbornness equal to hers, that he would not, for reasons that would remain his own, reveal his motives.

"However, I can assure you, madam, that this does not in any way concern my wife," he added. "Nor would the finding of this young woman adversely affect Juliana."

"Pah! You young people!" she said disdainfully. "Always seeking what you do not have."

With that, she leaned forward on her chair and looked him in the eye, wagging a tiny pointed finger in his direction.

"My Lord Pembroke, it is Juliana's happiness I seek, and if you are to be the instrument of it, you shall be blest. But," she said with a stern shake of her head, "if you are to add to her troubles, you shall be well and truly cursed."

Nicholas frowned, but not at the threat.

"Pray, madam, of what difficulties do you speak?" he said.

Mrs. Duville leaned back in her chair with a mournful look.

"The deaths of Juliana's parents—they perished in a carriage accident several years ago, you know—affected her greatly," she said. After a moment's hesitation she added, "Indeed, I begin to wonder if she will ever come about. She has taken it upon herself, you see, to avenge them."

Nicholas stroked his chin, evidence that he was pondering a thorny question. Then, when it became clear Mrs. Duville had no plan to continue, he spoke.

"But surely a coaching accident, though tragic, is a happenstance that could occur to anyone. What, pray, is there to avenge?" Nicholas said, puzzled.

"Ah, but that is it, you see," Mrs. Duville said and, leaning forward, continued in a dramatic whisper. "It was no accident! At least, Juliana believes it was not."

Startled, Nicholas pulled his chair closer.

"Pray, madam, I would hear the whole," he commanded gently.

Mrs. Duville gave him a measuring look and, seemingly satisfied with what she saw, began the story.

It was a tale that Nicholas pondered as he rode to London some hours later. According to Mrs. Duville, Juliana's mother Madeleine, who was French, and her father William fell deeply in love when they met in Paris. Madeleine, whom Elise Duville served, easily persuaded her father, a nobleman who was to lose his fortune and then his head during the Terror, to consent to the match with the wealthy English lord. They produced two children, Juliana and Robert, and had by every evidence led a loving and happy life at Lindenwood.

The marquess would not give up his work for the Foreign Office, however, and frequently embarked on rather mysterious and prolonged absences that were, of necessity, accepted in the family but never discussed. That he was a spy could not be doubted, Mrs. Duville insisted, and though she admired the marquess, she would forever fault him for not giving up such dangerous duty for the sake of his family.

It was in October 1807, a month after Britain had accomplished a bold raid that damaged Copenhagen and destroyed the Danish fleet—snatching it, in effect, from Napoleon's hand—that the marquess and his wife were killed in a carriage accident as they were returning to Lindenwood from London. Nicholas remembered the raid; it had rekindled hope for the enemies of the French Empire at a time when Napoleon was riding the high tide of conquest.

A faulty axle was deemed the cause of the accident, Mrs. Duville said, shaking her head in scornful disbelief. The marquess, it was widely known, had had a hand in the raid. Indeed, she confided, it was widely believed that he had planned it.

The family was plunged deeply into mourning, and Juliana had, of course, foregone the Season she was to have the next year. She became a virtual recluse at Lindenwood, and her brother Robert went abroad, where he now remained. Both of the marquess's children, it seemed, had vowed to avenge the murders, which they believed to have been ordered by the emperor himself.

Nicholas furrowed his brow in thought. He had learned nothing of his mystery woman, for as to that Mrs. Duville insisted she had nothing to reveal. But his wife was another matter, and he still remembered Nanny Duville's plaintive parting words to him:

"She has closed herself up inside, milord, and will not allow the light in."

James was sitting at the desk in his study, fingering some papers. This time Nicholas did him the courtesy of having himself announced, and so James was able to offer a friendly but guarded welcome. Any hope that Nicholas had put aside his efforts to locate his mystery woman were dashed by his first words.

"You might as well give over that complacent grin, James. I have not yet found her, but I will."

James sighed and gestured for Nicholas to take a chair.

"Let us not begin again, my friend. Nothing has changed, as you must know," James said.

Nicholas grinned.

"Only that you have not yet offered me a glass of your excellent brandy, and for that I might well take offense."

Delighted that their friendship again appeared to be on even ground, James obliged. There was nothing exceptional said until Nicholas drew the last swallow of his drink and set the glass on the desk with a thump.

"I might as well tell you, James, as I doubt word has traveled here yet. We have not yet sent notices to the papers. It was a quiet affair, necessitated by circumstances too complicated to mention."

"What portentous event is this?" James asked in amusement.

"It seems I have gotten myself leg-shackled, my friend, and to a woman who is no more desirous of having me as a husband than I am to have her as a wife," Nicholas responded, expelling a great breath.

James's mouth opened in shock, and his face, normally schooled into a mask of calm amiability, betrayed his astonishment. But that reaction paled to the one caused by Nicholas's next words:

"Yes, 'tis true. Lady Juliana Westlake and I were married Sunday fortnight and have settled at Seagate, my mother's childhood home, near Lindenwood."

James remained immobile; for once he could think of nothing to do or say. He opened his mouth to speak, but thought better of it, and clamped it shut again. The two men sat in silence for a time, each with his own rather depressing thoughts. Finally James spoke.

"You say neither of you desired the marriage?" he began slowly. "You will not take it amiss, then, if I say that I do not quite collect the circumstances. Lady Juliana is not unknown to me, and I have always judged her fully capable of ordering her own affairs."

"It was my fault that we were thrust into marriage," Nicholas said. "I believe her aunt, misapprehending a situation in which Lady Juliana and I found ourselves, rather forced the item onto the plate, so to speak. It would not be appropriate to go into greater detail. Suffice it to say that my wife's greatest concern seems to be that we remain at Seagate for the nonce."

Nicholas lifted his frame from the chair and, preparing to leave, gave his friend a pained look.

"It would be folly, my friend, to pretend that we are happy in this union. But I have hope that we at least will achieve some state of equilibrium. I believe, therefore, that it would be beneficial if there were others to . . . diffuse the situation, so to speak. Mayhap you will consider honoring us with a visit? I believe you said you were acquainted with my wife."

"Indeed, I have long known her family," James said cautiously. "The marquess, her father, was associated with the Foreign Office."

"Ah, yes. I believe he perished in rather mysterious circumstances, did he not?"

James shuffled some papers and studied the mantel clock as it began to chime the hour.

"On the contrary, I believe there was nothing extraordinary about it. 'Twas a carriage accident, I understand," he replied easily.

"Has no one ever suggested otherwise?" Nicholas asked. "Could the marquess's activities, for example, have provoked the emperor?"

"I cannot think that the lofty little Corsican would suffer himself to take such notice of an English lord as to order his murder," James said quickly.

"Murder?" Nicholas arched his brows and bestowed on his friend a grim expression. "That was your word, James, not mine."

The amber liquid sparkled in the candlelight, creating an interesting pattern as he swirled the glass and took yet another drink. Nicholas paid the barest intention to the game of whist that was being played at the table nearest his chair, for he had come to White's not to play, but to drink, and seriously.

It was not something he did as a rule, but Nicholas reflected that the glowing liquid did have the capacity to bring the troubling questions that had preoccupied his brain to happy surcease. It dulled the edge of his disappointment at the cold trail his spy had left behind. Likewise, it smoothed the uneasiness he felt when he thought of Juliana, a feeling that had sharpened since his visit with Mrs. Duville. He could not escape the notion that the marriage would only add to Juliana's difficulties. And he knew in chagrin that he had already done so with his unforgivable behavior. He could not fathom his actions for there was nothing at all enticing about his wife. Indeed, it had struck him that she was so far the opposite, she might have been engaging in a deliberate attempt to make herself appear dowdy. Those shapeless gowns, that severely pulled back hair, those unsightly mop caps—Nicholas shuddered at the image.

But just as quickly, another image appeared of her face, with its large green eyes and trembling mouth, the way it had looked when he kissed her. There was something vulnerable and appealing in Juliana, despite the sharp tongue that seemed to delight in making him its target. He often wondered what really went on in her brain. Perhaps he would never know.

"I understand congratulations are in order, old man! Allow me to stand a round! Nothing too good for the new bridegroom!"

Nicholas looked up into a face he could not immediately place. The swell wore a navy cutaway, floral crimson waistcoat and yellow breeches, at the top of which dangled nigh to a dozen fobs. Suspended from them were a diversity of plaques, stones, and a watch. He was peering at Nicholas through an ornate quizzing glass attached to a buttonhole and looking for all the world as if he had found a long-lost friend. Nicholas shook the cobwebs from his head and tried to put a name to the apparition.

"Sir Perceval Smythington at your service, my lord," the voice said with a smooth cheerfulness that bordered on unctuousness. "Oxford, remember? To be sure, I knew you right off, but as I collect that marriage has the capacity to addle the brain, I take the liberty of re-introducing myself."

Nicholas rose in a greeting, although he was not happy to have his meditations interrupted. He tried to recall the man, but the memory was vague and somehow did not warm him.

"I did not think the *Gazette* had been notified of the nuptials," Nicholas said.

"Nor do I know whether that is the case," replied Smythington smoothly. "I cannot think where I heard the news. Suffice it to say it is about. My felicitations. The Lady Juliana must make you a delightful and, may I say, *resourceful* bride."

Nicholas frowned, as he did not take the man's meaning. But he was just as eager to have him begone. Perhaps he himself ought to leave, now that he thought of it.

"You have met my wife?" Nicholas queried absently, unable to banish the tantalizing image of his wife as she had looked when he kissed her.

"To be sure, and one would never forget such a lady," Smythington effused. "Although I doubt whether she remembers the pup that I was when we met at a rout some years ago."

At Nicholas's puzzled look, he continued.

"I am all eagerness to renew the acquaintance, however. It happens that some of my set remove to Brighton shortly, and it would not be out of the way to call," Smythington said pleasantly. "That is to say, if it would not be inconvenient?"

But Nicholas had already summoned an attendant with his hat and gloves, and in his eagerness to quit the scene paid Smythington little mind.

"What? Yes, yes, pleasure, to be sure. You must excuse me now. I have an engagement," Nicholas said, and hastily took his leave.

Nicholas decided he couldn't help it if Sir Perceval thought his excuse contrived. He could never explain the real reason—that he had an uncontrollable urge to see his wife.

9

I have deceived even your very eyes.
—SHAKESPEARE, *Much Ado About Nothing*

IT WAS NOT until two days after Nicholas's return to Seagate
that he located his wife. Juliana was not at home the day he
arrived, nor indeed the next. She had left word with Mrs.
Burling that she was visiting Mrs. Duville, and with that
Nicholas supposed he was to be satisfied.

But the sight of his countess as she crossed the threshold
late on the afternoon of the third day was far from satisfy-
ing. Nicholas had never seen her looking so bedraggled and
fatigued. Her black riding habit was untidy and wrinkled. Her
hair appeared to have been hastily stuffed under a riding hat
that perched precariously on her head. But that was not the
worst of it. Her eyes were red, as if she had not slept, and
the left side of her face wore a bluish bruise. She looked,
if such an appellation could be applied to the daughter of a
marquess, like the devil himself.

When Juliana saw Nicholas, her eyes widened in alarm.

"Why are you not in London?" she said with a gasp, and
then teetered unsteadily.

A startled footman rushed to her aid, but Nicholas arrived
at her side first. He scooped Juliana into his massive arms
and carried her up to her chamber where he placed her
gently on the bed. After assuring himself she appeared in

no need of immediate medical attention, he rang impatiently for her maid.

"A bath and then bed for your mistress," he commanded the frightened girl, who bobbed him a quick, nervous curtsy. She let out a shriek, however, when she saw Juliana's appearance.

Nicholas crossed the chamber to leave his wife to her maid's ministrations. As he reached the doorway, he turned and looked at Juliana's reclining figure and dazed expression. He stroked his chin thoughtfully and, without a word, left the room.

Juliana paused outside the door of Nicholas's study. She had not awakened until late morning, and it was nearly time for nuncheon. But she was unable to bear the thought of facing her husband over the table without first bearding the lion in his den. She patted her hair and smoothed the lavender lawn that looked, she supposed, as well as anything in her wardrobe.

Tears welled in Juliana's eyes as she thought of her fruitless trip. She had prayed mightily that this journey would at last bring her brother home. They had had reason to believe that Napoleon, holding Saxony at the Elbe River, was weighing a new offensive involving troops near Dresden. Robert, who had infiltrated the French command, was to bring word of the plan and then return with her to England. They were to meet at the tavern. But, Juliana reflected bitterly, England's victory was her loss. French fortunes now had begun collapsing in Spain with Wellington's great victory at Vitoria. The emperor, knowing his empire was in mortal danger, was playing a waiting game.

And so Juliana had returned empty-handed and exhausted from France after waiting at the tavern for three days. And although Mrs. Duville's cousin Michele had looked after her, as he always did, Juliana was never at ease. Once she had tripped and fallen as she sought to evade an amorous patron. She touched the bruise on her face gingerly and shook her head. This was a dangerous charade, and she heartily wished the end of it.

Juliana grimaced. She had been horrified to see Nicholas standing in the hall on her return with Peters. Whatever did he think? She put her hand on the door and resolutely pushed it open.

Nicholas looked up from his desk at the person of his wife. She looked tolerably well, he thought, at least by comparison with yesterday.

"I hope I am not intruding," Juliana said quietly.

"Not at all," Nicholas said, putting his papers aside and rising to meet her. "My concentration has eluded me this morning, at all events."

Juliana accepted Nicholas's arm as he assisted her into a chair near the window. He remained standing and studied her face, and she found she could not return his steadfast gaze.

"I see you are more yourself today. I hope you slept well," he said in a voice betraying nothing but polite concern.

"Yes, quite," Juliana replied briskly, smoothing her skirt. "That is, I am quite myself today, thank you."

There was a prolonged silence during which Nicholas leaned back against the desk, fixing his eyes on her face in a way that she found unnerving. She forced herself to return his unblinking gaze, but she could not bring herself to speak and eventually looked away. Finally Nicholas cleared his throat.

"I am wondering if you would care to tell me what happened," he said simply.

Juliana took a deep breath.

"I went to visit Elise Duville, you know," she began, focusing on her hands clasped tightly on her lap.

"Yes, Mrs. Burling so informed me, although I confess I would rather have liked a note in your hand with perhaps more information, such as the prospective length of your stay," Nicholas responded quietly.

Juliana looked up quickly, but his face offered no animosity.

"Well, I did not think of that, as I am not used to accounting for my activities, and when I got there, I found that Elise was so very ill," Juliana said, rising from her chair and beginning to pace. Absentmindedly wringing the handkerchief she held, Juliana paused at the window and said in a voice that she fervently hoped was sincerity itself:

"I simply could not leave her, and she required day and night attendance. I'm afraid I never thought of sending for help or additional clothes. I left her in much better condition yesterday, but I am afraid I was exhausted by the ordeal."

Juliana looked at Nicholas whose face was unreadable. Soundlessly joining her at the window, he gently touched his finger to her discolored cheek.

"And this?" he asked quietly.

"Oh!" She gave a nervous laugh. "I was so tired on the way back I'm afraid I took a turn too sharply and fell off my horse."

She shot him an embarrassed smile.

"I would have thought that your groom would have been more watchful in preventing such an occurrence." Nicholas might have been commenting on the weather for all the casualness in his voice.

"Well, Peters knows I like him to keep his distance. He is really along for form's sake, you know, as I much prefer to ride alone," she replied too quickly.

"And yet I observed him constantly in your presence when you went off on your rides at Lindenwood," Nicholas persisted gently. "And although you and I have not yet ridden together, I have never formed the impression that you are an indifferent horsewoman."

"I suppose when one is exhausted, one does not perform

as one is accustomed," she said, seating herself again with a final, challenging arch of her brow.

The silence lengthened. Juliana, feeling that she would do well if he believed even one word of her tale, sat with her hands folded in a show of outward calm. Nicholas stared at a point on the wall above her head and rubbed his chin thoughtfully.

"I know," he said finally, "that our arrangement provides each of us an unusual measure of independence, but I am wondering if we have not both been guilty of ill judgment."

Juliana cocked her head at him and then colored as Nicholas pulled a chair close to hers. Leaning over, he took one of her hands, and Juliana felt his eyes bore into her.

"Even though there is no pretense of marital affection between us," he said gently, "I believe that for the reasons of prudence, harmony, and consideration, we had ought to better advise the other of our comings and goings."

Juliana wanted to look away but found she could not.

"I should not have taken myself off to London without informing you personally. Though I had no fixed notion of the length of my stay, it would have been better to acquaint you with that myself rather than leaving word with the housekeeper," Nicholas said.

She looked at him in surprise, and he smiled before his face grew quite serious.

"Perhaps you would be kind enough to do the same in the future. For it is not so much your independence I wish to curtail as it is your safety I wish to preserve," Nicholas said. "You are, after all, under the protection of my name. It is a responsibility I do not mean to avoid."

He squeezed her hands warmly and touched her chin lightly with his fingertips.

"Despite the nature of our arrangement, I would not like anything to happen to you, Juliana," he said softly. "And yesterday you gave me quite a fright."

Juliana felt herself tingle at his touch. She pulled her face back quickly and tore her eyes from his.

"I will endeavor to be more thoughtful in the future, my lord," she said briskly, and rose hastily to leave. Nicholas silently watched her cross the room.

"Juliana," Nicholas said as she reached the door. She turned at his voice.

"Yes, my lord?"

"Do you think perhaps you might call me Nicholas?" he asked politely. "It is my given name, after all."

Juliana looked up at the pewter eyes that glimmered with the merest ghost of a smile.

"Yes, my . . . Nicholas," she replied, and fled.

The garden off the terrace had become one of Juliana's favorite places. During Nicholas's absence, she had found time to follow the winding paths that meandered down to the beach. Though the garden had over the years deteriorated into an overgrown patch of unrestrained growth, Nicholas had rescued it from long disuse. The effect, Juliana reflected as she walked aimlessly along a handsome row of fruit trees, was quite pleasant.

She was thankful that it was not one of those formal constructions. They were acceptable for town but really looked quite foolish in the country, she thought, letting her mind ramble. And although she admired the French style of radial avenues, canals, parterres and the like, she personally favored a less authoritarian approach. And so exploring this delightfully tamed but natural expanse had become a pleasant ritual. She loved the sinuous graveled walks that led from the terrace through casually grouped shrubberies, flowerbeds, pear trees, and cedars. Nearer the beach, the path descended into stone walkways and small stone bridges that traversed some of the more substantial outcroppings.

It was peaceful here, Juliana thought, as she passed the old greenhouse that had not yet had the benefit of restoration. Though it had once been handsome, it was now almost sinister looking, its unblinking windows long since grown into blank rows of unseeing dark eyes. Once Juliana had imagined that those eyes stared back at her, and she gave an inadvertent shudder at the almost palpable air of malice.

Today, however, she gave the greenhouse little thought as she skirted it quickly and headed down the path to the beach. She was contemplating her husband's request that she better acquaint him with her actions. It was a reasonable demand, she supposed, and although he had not couched it in those terms, she sensed he meant to enforce it. He could have no objections to continuing her visits with Elise, however, and he need not know that the little cottage provided only a stopover for exchanging her regular garments for "Marie's" tattered frock.

She was less disturbed over this possible complication to her plans than by the knowledge that her husband's capacity to throw her into a tizzy was growing almost daily. There was no denying that her pulse beat a little faster in Nicholas's presence, her normally civil tongue deserted her, and her poised self-confidence evaporated. Only a timid mouse would have fled at the simple request that she use his given name, and Juliana knew herself not to be such a pitiful creature. She was still frowning over her behavior during yesterday's disconcerting interview, when she heard a twig snap.

"I hope you are enjoying the garden, Juliana," Nicholas said in the deep baritone that was becoming most familiar.

"Indeed, my lord," she replied with a deliberately careless air, "I believe that Mr. Addison was wont to call it one of the most innocent delights in human life."

"I thought we were at 'Nicholas.' I do hope I have not fallen back to 'my lord,' " he said gravely.

Juliana laughed to cover her discomposure and delivered

a response with a jauntiness she was far from feeling.

"If you have fallen, sir, 'tis in your own estimation, for I assure you that my memory needs but a jog to set things aright. 'Nicholas' you shall be henceforth."

"And you, Juliana, have reminded me of Mr. Addison's remarks, which I cannot help but think were in the mind of my forebear when this garden was designed," Nicholas replied easily.

"I collect you are referring to his belief that the garden should be a place to fill the mind with calmness and tranquility," she said.

"Yes, and to 'lay all its turbulent passions at rest,' " Nicholas finished.

Juliana said nothing. Nicholas studied her closed profile.

"Madam, are you perhaps troubled by any turbulence that you care to share?"

The words startled her, and she gave a half laugh that sounded false even to her own ears.

"Nay, my . . . Nicholas, for I cannot like the notion of one's sound good judgment being subject to the unpredictability of such disruptive forces," she said with forced gaiety. "You may be sure I shall never allow *that* to trouble me."

"A wise choice, to be sure, Juliana," Nicholas replied. "Perhaps you might be good enough to tell me just how it is you have learned to master the more volatile aspects of human nature. Surely many have long sought such a gift as you have. Although you will forgive me for the observation that during our brief acquaintance you seem at times to find your gift . . . elusive."

Juliana gave him an assessing sideways glance.

"You may jest if you like, Nicholas, but 'tis a simple matter of necessity, is it not? One has one's duty in life after all, and surely that is always to be uppermost in one's mind."

"And what is that duty, Juliana, to which you enjoy such obligation?" he asked softly.

She moved ahead of him on the path in order to negotiate an overhanging branch as she pondered a response. The silence had stretched considerably before she found one.

"One's duty is, of course, to one's family and country, my lord, although I suppose some would say that one's name and position hold the higher trust," she said.

"And you do not?"

"One's name and position are simply accidents of birth, are they not? I suppose they command a certain amount of loyalty, and those of us who are fortunate enough to be well-born should be thankful, to be sure," Juliana responded. "But I cannot think that service to one's title should supplant that higher duty to protect and provide for family and country."

Nicholas moved to her side, and they walked along a section of path sheltered by large cedars that towered like giant soldiers guarding their turf. The lush growth encased them in its silence. Finally Nicholas spoke.

"It is unusual, Juliana, to hear a female speak thus. Your parents must have been extraordinary people to rear you with such notions. Or did you, perhaps, acquire them on your own?"

Juliana searched his eyes to see if he was mocking her. Satisfied that he was not, she responded.

"My parents were indeed extraordinary, my lord, and I suppose they did put some unusual notions in my head. However, my mind has been my own now for quite some time, and I believe I must presume that my beliefs are likewise."

Nicholas smiled as she finished speaking and gently put his hand under her arm to guide her past a jutting rock.

"I had never a doubt, madam," he said gravely.

They walked past a grove of smaller cedars that served as the last buffer between the garden and the sea. The path wound more steeply down at this point, and the silence lengthened into a companionable interlude as they concentrated on their steps. Finally Nicholas shattered the mood.

"How did your parents die, Juliana?"

She missed a step as she jerked her head up to see if she had heard him aright. His arm reached out and supported her as he calmly returned her stare. She took a deep breath.

" 'Twas a carriage accident," she said, forcing her feet to concentrate on negotiating the rocks that had overtaken the smooth gravel.

"What happened?" he asked, and held out his hand to help her over a large stone.

"A broken axle," she said in a constricted voice, and then looked up at him with a tight smile. "I suppose I attract them."

Nicholas looked at her in puzzlement.

"But you were not in the carriage, surely?"

Her face was impassive, but Nicholas saw her eyelids flutter as if she were trying to hold back tears.

"No," she replied finally, her voice perfectly controlled, "I was not."

The path abruptly became steeper, and they had to hold onto the brush to retain their footing. They followed the path in single file as it wound down to a smooth expanse of sand that disappeared into the frothy blue-green of the water.

Juliana, trying to recover her equanimity, cast her eyes to the horizon. For the first time she noticed a boat bobbing off-shore near the dock that lay a quarter-mile beyond them.

"What a handsome yacht," she said. "I do not believe I know it."

" 'Tis mine, actually," Nicholas replied, accepting her change of subject. "I had it brought down from Harwich, thinking perhaps it might prove a pleasant diversion since we remain here for the summer." He thought it was just as well not to mention he had also weighed its usefulness for a possible trip across the channel.

Juliana studied the sleek lines of the craft as it was lifted by the waves. She could not make out its name.

"Pray, what do you call it?" she said.

"Lord Haversham—he owned it before I, you know— christened it the *Sea Witch,* but I am contemplating changing it, for I find that commonplace," he said.

"To what, pray?"

Nicholas looked beyond the boat to the deeper waters that separated England and France.

"I have not yet been inspired with a better name," he said, "but I have always had a fondness for *Marie.*"

The sound of the crashing waves nearly took his words, and their thunder echoed the pounding of Juliana's heart.

The hand, encased in a black kid glove, held a pistol to Robert's head. Her brother was blindfolded and sat silently as a voice laughed from somewhere with malevolent glee. Juliana had a pistol of her own, but it was heavy, so heavy, and she could not bring it to a firing position. Indeed her whole body seemed to be weighted as with lead, and she could barely move. She wanted to warn him, but when she opened her mouth, no sound emerged. She saw the gloved hand clench and a finger begin to squeeze the trigger.

"No!" she cried as she threw her body with all her might at the unseen gunman. But there was nothing there— only air—and she felt herself falling, falling into a black chasm of evil and despair. She opened her mouth and screamed.

The arms caught her then. She thrashed against them, but they held her fast, and gradually she ceased to struggle.

"Juliana!"

The word pierced through the fog that swirled about her brain, and she suddenly entered another world, one in which worried blue-grey eyes stared down at her and a pair of massive arms rocked her soothingly.

"Juliana! 'Tis but a nightmare. You are here in your room. All is well."

Juliana's dazed eyes focused on her husband, and she realized that he was holding her to his chest. The bedclothes were tangled, and her gown was twisted and soaked with perspiration.

"Nicholas!" She pushed her body away from him. "I must have made a terrible racket, I suppose."

He smiled. "No more than anyone else in the throes of a nightmare. I heard you as I passed your chamber on the way to mine."

She looked at him in confusion. He was fully dressed.

"But I thought you retired when I did. It must be late, surely?"

Nicholas had risen to leave, and he turned back toward the figure silhouetted against the moonlit window. The chamber was so dark that her voice seemed to come from the shadows, and he shook his head to clear the image of the woman who suddenly appeared in his mind.

"I found I was not sleepy after all," he said. "But now I think it best that we both try for a good rest. That is, if you think you are quite recovered?"

The figure seemed oddly forlorn as it studied him.

"Yes, thank you, Nicholas. I am perfectly fine."

He turned his back then and shut the door, pausing for a moment outside the chamber. Had he imagined the quiver in her voice?

It was when he was walking to the stables the next day that he heard the shots. They came from the direction of the ha-ha on the edge of the field behind the stables, and he grabbed a whip and ran toward the sounds. As they grew louder, Nicholas saw a figure positioned some hundred yards from the fence, on which were arranged an assortment of bottles, twigs, and jars. As he advanced, Nicholas recognized the figure as Juliana, who was calmly firing a set of pistols as Peters reloaded. Nicholas watched as Juliana narrowed her eyes, pointed the gun, and squeezed the trigger. A twig that had been tied to the fence snapped in two.

"I did not know you were such a crack shot, madam," he said, startling her into a tiny jump. Peters gave him a wary look.

Juliana smiled in greeting.

"Actually, I am sadly out of practice, Nicholas. Should you care to have a friendly contest?"

He returned her smile, surprised at her cordiality and glad to hear his name on her lips.

"Nay, for I know when I have met my match. I shall simply rest here at your feet, my lady, and watch you at your art." With that he plopped down in the grass and looked up at her mischievously. He saw with satisfaction that her face, lined from lack of sleep, broke immediately into another smile.

"Silly man! You think to make me miss, do you not? I should warn you that my nerves do not rattle so easily!"

She took a pistol from Peters, raised it to the target, and shattered a tiny vinaigrette bottle perched on the fence.

Nicholas applauded loudly.

"Well done, madam! It seems that in extending you the protection of my name, I have, ironically, acquired a protector. I delight in the knowledge and am pleased to know I may sleep easy in my bed now!"

Juliana gave a mock frown and sat down beside him.

"I am sure you need not go on so, my lord, for I have every confidence that you are quite capable of protecting yourself if the need should arise," she said sternly.

"Is that what this is all about?" His face suddenly grew serious. "Are you afraid of something, Juliana?"

She flushed and looked at him in irritation and, he thought, embarrassment.

"Why must you always take a pleasant conversation and

turn it into an inquisition?" she demanded. "I simply enjoy shooting, and that, sir, is that!"

She turned her head so he could not see her eyes, but the tremble of her lip betrayed her. Nicholas reached up and put his arm around her shoulders.

"I would not question your pleasure, Juliana, nor seek to cast a pall upon it," he said softly. "But I do wish to know if there is something troubling you."

She held herself rigid against the concern she heard in his voice. Drat the man! She would rather have him at fisticuffs with her than as he was now—his face a mask of solicitude and his penetrating eyes searching hers for their secrets.

Frostily she met his direct gaze.

"As I told you last night, sir, I am perfectly fine."

Nicholas stroked his chin as he studied her closed countenance. The sunlight picked up the highlights in her hair, and yet it did nothing to dispel the atmosphere of darkness he sensed about her spirit in that moment.

"There is nothing wrong with my hearing, Juliana," he said softly, idly flicking a blade of grass off her skirt. "Only just remember that, whatever the eccentricities of our arrangement, I am your husband. I expect that you will turn to me if you are in difficulty."

She gave him a sidelong look but said nothing.

"You know, I am just beginning to realize, my dear," he continued, turning the full force of his pewter eyes on her, "what an interesting arrangement this is."

10

August 1813

~◆~

Friendship is constant in all other things
save in the office and affairs of love.
—SHAKESPEARE, *Much Ado About Nothing*

"LA, MY DEAR! This room will be just the thing for the ball—that is, if Lord Pembroke can have his workmen fix it up a bit," Lady Hereford said, looking with distaste at the dust that settled on the tip of her kid glove as it brushed the wall.

"As it happens, Aunt, this is the last of the rooms to be refurbished, and as you can see, the work is almost done," Juliana said, leading her aunt and cousin Sarah to the morning room.

Lady Hereford settled onto an ebony settee and adjusted her skirts, smiling approvingly at Sarah who was dressed in a silvery blue walking dress trimmed with pink ribands.

"I am so happy that you and *dear* Nicholas agreed to my suggestion to hold a ball in honor of your marriage," Lady Hereford said, smiling in great satisfaction. "You are these six weeks married, and I don't mind telling you, the manner in which you wed has set tongues wagging."

"I am sure the circumstances of my wedding are no one's

concern but my own." Juliana bristled.

Lady Hereford, thinking not for the first time that her niece had a remarkable lack of appreciation for Society's sensibilities, ignored the remark and continued.

"To be sure, it is all to the good that Sarah will be a beneficiary of your celebration, as she will no doubt meet many eligible young gentlemen who have not had the opportunity to feast their eyes on her this long summer!"

"Oh, Mama!" Sarah exclaimed in embarrassment. "I am sure it is not my wish to meet any such gentlemen!"

"Nonsense! All young women wish it," Lady Hereford responded quellingly. "And I am certain that Lord Pembroke has not a few acquaintances who, happily, will broaden our circle and show you, my dear, the merits of a *true* gentleman."

As this was apparently a pointed reference to a certain squire's son, it threw the room into an awkward silence. Sarah plunged into the sullens. Juliana eyed her aunt in consternation. Lady Hereford merely smiled benignly.

Any further conversation was, in any event, halted by the butler's announcement of Sir James, who had finally accepted Nicholas's invitation to visit with an eagerness tempered by trepidation and exacerbated by a certain amount of morbid fascination.

As his arrival had been expected, Juliana was able to rise calmly to greet James and Nicholas. None of the four noticed Lady Hereford's reaction, which could best be described as the sort of predatory ecstasy found in the household cat when it has sighted the hapless creature that will become dinner.

For as Lady Hereford surveyed James, he gave every evidence of being a veritable tulip of fashion, a pink of the *ton*, a nob in fine trim.

His lithe frame was adorned in a morning coat that, while unremarkable in itself, topped a puce waistcoat on which a florid pattern was embroidered in crimson. His buff doeskin pantaloons clung snugly to his well-formed limbs which were encased in crimson-striped stockings. He carried a carved yewwood cane with a gold-encrusted parrot's head handle. The distinctively balanced starcher he wore at the neck gave his chin a superior tilt that somehow remained so even as he bowed low to the beaming Lady Hereford.

"Well, I was just telling my daughter Sarah—dear, *do* come over here and greet Sir James!—that Lord Pembroke undoubtedly was blessed with friends of no small consequence," Lady Hereford gushed. "And indeed I see that I was not in error! To be sure, we are delighted to know you, sir!"

James bowed again, clasping the proffered tips of Lady Hereford's fingers and smiling at Sarah, who blushed to the tips of her toes.

"And I am equally delighted to have the thingular honor of making your acquaintanceth," he replied, his lisp more pronounced than Nicholas could ever recall. Juliana stared at James with an incredulous arch of her brow. But their reactions were lost in Lady Hereford's single-minded assault upon their guest.

She had somehow managed to vacate the settee, which then came to be occupied by her daughter and, by dint of Lady Hereford's maneuvering, Sir James himself. Although Sarah seemed to be tongue-tied, no such fate befell her aunt who spent the better part of a quarter hour waxing ecstatically in delighted anticipation of the ball. When she learned that James intended to remain the fortnight until the happy event, there were no bounds to her exuberance. Indeed, she was so reluctant to quit Seagate that, had Juliana not secured from her a promise to return with Sarah for the evening meal, Lady Hereford might well have remained until then.

The Seagate party was increased by two more guests by dinner time as, to the amazement of Nicholas and the bewilderment of Juliana, Sir Perceval Smythington and his sister, Lady Iphigene Torrent, arrived on their doorstep that very afternoon. The coach that brought their bags contained so many trunks and parcels that Juliana was afraid to contemplate what it portended until Sir Perceval explained that they were on their way to Brighton for what remained of the summer.

"And of course we just had to stop here—thanks to Lord Pembroke's kind invitation!—to offer our felicitations and renew our acquaintance," Perceval said as he clasped Juliana's hands and looked into her startled face. His face took on a hurt expression when his reminder that they had met several years ago at a London rout brought no smile of recognition to her face, as indeed, Juliana could not recall ever going to a London rout. She did not wish to appear rude, however, and so let the matter drop.

Dinner was a lively affair. James found himself positioned between Sarah and her mother, with Perceval placed to Juliana's right and Iphigene to Nicholas's left. There was nothing remarkable about those arrangements, indeed they suited everyone except for the hostess, whose own seating plan was surreptitiously changed just before dinner by her aunt so that James would be placed next to Sarah rather than at Juliana's right.

Throughout dinner, Sir Perceval hung on Juliana's every word. He favored her with so many speaking glances and admiring phrases for her appearance—which she knew was no better than usual—that she was quite bewildered as to his purpose and not a little uncomfortable.

Nicholas, at the other end of the table, received similar treatment from Lady Iphigene, a blond beauty whose good looks and rather ample charms were given more than adequate display by her ivory sarcenet gown with a square neckline cut precariously low. Lady Iphigene was a widow, her elderly miser of a husband having done her the favor of sticking his spoon in the wall some few months after their marriage. There was nothing miserly, however, about the diamonds that she wore about her neck and which were rumored to have been the parting gift of a Corinthian who, happily, found a more enjoyable manner in ~~which to spend his~~ time than in the company of such a sharp-set ladybird; for Lady Iphigene had a way of peering down her angular nose with steely blue eyes in a look that usually preceded one of her famous displays of temper and which invariably created the necessity of producing another trinket to mollify her.

In short, Lady Iphigene was casting about for another protector, and her lures had Nicholas firmly in view.

Juliana found she could not help but notice the blandishments the lady employed, her delicate fingers often touching Nicholas's sleeve and her eyelashes fluttering in dainty appreciation of his every remark. If Lady Iphigene leaned over any further in Nicholas's direction, her diamonds would surely be in his plate, Juliana thought. Her husband, she observed, was far from finding the lady's efforts unappealing. She saw that his face often broke into an odd sort of smile that seemed to carry a wealth of meaning when coupled with the degree of warmth conveyed by his eyes.

James, she saw, was playing a cool game with Sarah and Lady Hereford, having trotted out every fulsome expression in his repertoire to express his delight at being in their presence but somehow, she thought, managing to avoid giving the impression that he was an easy pigeon to pluck.

"My *dear* Sir James," Lady Hereford was saying. "You must give us all the news from town, for I do declare that we get nothing at all, and I have been *famished* for gossip. Why, I never even got an account of the princess's appearance at King's Theater!"

"I assure you, my lady, that had you been there, your breath would have been quite taken away," James said. "Not only was there Catalani, of course, who shone with more than her accustomed brilliance, but Her Royal Highness herself did not appear until well into the performance. You can well imagine the air of expectation, not to mention the wagers offered in the pit, over her first public appearance since the . . . ah, attempts upon her honor!"

Lady Hereford held her fork suspended between her mouth and plate as James's words held her rapt.

"When she did appear, she was preceded by Lady Charlotte Campbell—and you will appreciate this, ma'am—who was decorated with flowers *à la française*. Every eye focused on the royal box—Lord Castlereagh was in a box four or five from the princess, you know—and there were—well, I can only describe them as peals of joy at the princess's appearance. She received it all with much self-composure, though evidently forcibly impressed with the touching interest of the audience."

James sat back in his chair to dab a napkin at his mouth. Lady Hereford looked at him eagerly.

"But her appearance, Sir James! Surely one with such powers of observation as yourself noted *that*!" she urged.

"To be sure, madam. Indeed, the princess looked in very good health, although she appeared rather more pale than usual. She was dressed in mourning, with a white veil thrown over her shoulders, and her headdress was adorned simply with a Greek bandeau of diamonds. She bowed gracefully to the audience and appeared manifestly affected by all those fine feelings which were, I am certain, reassuring as to the public faith in her innocence and virtue," James finished with a broad flourish of his hand.

"Although," he added after the long pause in which his audience absorbed these details, "there was heard here and there a hiss!"

"No!" Lady Hereford said with a gasp.

"I'm afraid it is true," James replied mournfully. "For faith in our princesseth character is not, I am forced to say, univerthal."

As Juliana watched her aunt's wide-eyed expression, she vowed to say something to James privately about that disgusting lisp, which she knew was all the crack among the dandies but to her seemed fatuous.

At her elbow Sir Perceval was attempting to catch her attention.

"Well, my lady, I am confident that you, like many of our happy countrymen and women, are relieved that peace is at hand at last," he said with an insinuating smile.

"Peace? Whatever can you mean?" Juliana said in surprise.

"Why, the armistice, as everyone knows, has been extended until the tenth. Surely one can hope for a more permanent cessation of hostilities," Perceval replied easily.

"You can have no understanding of the situation, my lord, if you believe that lasting peace will come from this charade," Juliana said impatiently.

"Oh? Perhaps you can enlighten me, for it is rare that I find ladies in my circle who are knowledgeable about continental affairs—beyond, that is, whether the latest silks are available yet from Paris," he said in a smooth voice.

Juliana made no immediate response, but their conversation had caught more than one set of ears around the table, and it was James who spoke.

"On the contrary, Sir Perceval, for I have often found many ladies of the realm more than a little informed of continental affairs. It is often we men who disthplay a remarkable ignorance and lack of understanding of the events that have affected the security of our lives and homes for lo these many years."

Perceval was unable to suppress a look of irritation, but he turned smoothly back to Juliana.

"Pray, madam, I see I have wronged you. Perhaps you will share with the table your view of the prospects of peace. Are you, perhaps, among those who believe that the emperor has another offensive up his sleeve?"

But James interrupted again.

"Would that not depend, Sir Perceval, on whether one believes—as the French seem to—that the ruin of England is quite practicable, if not through direct invasion, surely by a gradual waste of her resources? Under those circumstances, it would not pay to become too complacent about the emperor's plans, surely?"

Perceval's eyes narrowed.

"I am certain we must all be interested in your views, Sir James, but as you have admonished me to think more highly of the ladies' impressions, pray let us hear what our hostess thinks."

Juliana's eyes flashed and as she brought her gaze over to Perceval, she saw that her husband was surveying the three of them with attentiveness and something else she could not precisely make out. It was almost as if he were pondering less what was said than what had gone unsaid. He met her look and allowed his mouth to form an unfathomable half-smile.

But Juliana had had quite enough of this dinner and rose to signal the ladies to withdraw.

"I am certain that our table can have little interest in my views on such a subject," Juliana said briskly. "And you gentlemen surely are eager for your port."

She left the room, followed reluctantly by the other ladies and the eyes of every man, each pondering his private thoughts about the Lady Juliana.

It was decided that all parties would welcome a beach excursion, and accordingly, the Seagate contingent, joined by Sarah—Lady Hereford, deeming her adequately chaperoned by Juliana and Nicholas, remained at home to make the numbers even—set out for a ride and picnic along the sandy shore that formed the southern boundary of Seagate and neighboring Lindenwood.

James and Juliana had elected to travel on horseback, leaving Nicholas and Perceval with the necessity of accompanying the ladies Iphigene and Sarah in the landau, an arrangement that would not have been to Lady Hereford's liking if she had but known of it.

Nicholas had looked askance at his wife when she eagerly accepted James's invitation to ride out, but as she had not consulted him about the matter, Nicholas offered no objection and merely handed Lady Iphigene into the landau. For her part, Juliana saw with irritation the slight misstep that caused Iphigene to trip gracefully and fall back into Nicholas's arms.

"My dear Lady Iphigene," Juliana purred, "I do urge you to watch your step, as it would not do to have you confined to your bed with injury for the duration of your visit with us. We would so miss your lovely presence."

That comment having drawn a disapproving look from her husband, Juliana turned her horse alongside James's.

"That was poorly done," James said in amusement after they were out of earshot.

"Nonsense, James. It was not, as you well know," Juliana retorted.

"But, my dear, one would think you were jealous of the lady, when, as I have been reliably informed by your husband, your marriage is one of mere convenience," James said quietly, and had the satisfaction of seeing Juliana color.

"And indeed," he continued with a calculating look at his companion, "knowing your own sentiments about marriage, I confess I was shocked beyond words to learn that you had entered into that happy state."

Juliana slowed her mount.

"There was no choice, James!" she said in exasperation. "My aunt would have forced me to remove from Lindenwood, and you of all people know how important it is for me to remain here within easy shot of France."

"The Juliana I am most familiar with has never been forced by anyone to do anything against her will," James replied, casting her a sidelong look.

"Perhaps not, but the Juliana you knew is nigh exhausted from the strain of her double life, and her wherewithal is not what it once was," she said with a sigh.

"Perhaps it would be best if we bring this dangerous game to a halt," James said. "The fact of your marriage complicates matters enormously, in any event. I have long tried to dissuade you from the risks you have taken. Robert can take care of himself, you know, and there will be others to help him."

Juliana shook her head.

"No, James, I must see this through. And my marriage has naught to do with it," she said. "Nicholas and I have an understanding by which we each have our independence. He suspects nothing, you know, and I have no fear from that corner."

"Then you are a fool," James said roughly. "He is the one most likely to find you out."

Juliana spurred her horse, not liking James to think her shaken by his words. He followed suit, and they raced to a large rock a quarter-mile away. They both reached the point at the same time, and Juliana dismounted, laughing.

"You are too serious, James, as I have been intending to tell you," she teased. "Every time I listen to you with that horrid lisp I want to throw up my hands and roar. You are coming it too brown, you know, with your efforts to present to the world the image of the perfect fop! I am sure that no one who knows you is fooled."

"Ah, my dear, but I am not trying to fool those who know me," he responded with a superior elevation of his brow. "And I will not allow you to change the subject. Come and sit with me on this rock, for you know my leg will not allow me to keep up with your pace."

They sat on the edge of the stone, and James took Juliana's hands and fixed her with an uncharacteristically earnest look.

"Juliana, if you have been married to Nicholas for nearly two months and do not know that he is a persistent, stubborn man of considerable intellect, I believe you have misjudged him," he said.

"You are right on that score, James, for I do not know my husband at all," Juliana said, pulling one hand away to rub her temple. "Still, I hope I do not presume on our friendship to the extent that you believe me to be asking you for advice as to my marriage. That is a matter between Nicholas and me."

"And me, my dear, for if one of my most valuable agents is in danger, it is my concern."

"I am in no danger from my husband," Juliana retorted.

"And there you are wrong, Juliana," James said quietly. "Nicholas is seeking you and, I predict, will find you out. I tried to warn you in my note weeks ago, but you apparently paid no heed."

"He seeks another woman and in no way associates her with me," Juliana insisted.

James put one hand on Juliana's shoulder in a fatherly gesture.

"It occurs to me that you have no clue as to why Nicholas is searching for his mysterious spy. Let me enlighten you, then. It is not mere curiosity. It is because she fascinated him and fired his imagination. Perhaps she even touched his heart. I have seen him when he talks of her, and I can tell you that he will not let her go."

Juliana resolutely fixed her gaze on the sea.

"And has it never occurred to you," James added, "that at some point the woman that he seeks and the woman to whom he is married will become one in his mind?"

"Nonsense!" Juliana laughed dismissively. "Nicholas is no more attracted to me than I am to that idiot Perceval. I go to great lengths to make my appearance as unremarkable as possible."

James laughed scornfully.

"Think you that appearance disguises what comes from the heart?" He shook his head in a mock theatrical gesture. "What folly we mortals commit when we try to order emotions according to the dictates of the intellect!"

A stirring in the brush caused them both to look up. Nicholas was surveying them from his great height. His expression was unreadable, and he gave no sign as to whether he had heard James's last words. He did, however, look pointedly at James's hand where it rested on Juliana's shoulder. Juliana scrambled to her feet guiltily, while James looked blandly at his friend.

"You gave us a start, Nicholas! One would hardly think that one of your size could walk with the stealth of a cat," he said.

"I was merely eager to see, my friend, whether you had discovered the perfect spot for picnicking and were keeping it all to yourselves," Nicholas responded quietly. "And I see, moreover, that your position goes wanting—some shade, that is. May I suggest that we all remove to that tree nearby where the others wait?"

Juliana saw that the landau containing the party had pulled up to the shady area and that its occupants were eyeing them with interest.

"Forgive us, my lord, as, in renewing our acquaintance, we lost track of the time," said Juliana. "How . . . fortunate that you were so nearby."

"I am never very far away, Juliana," Nicholas warned quietly in his wife's ear, as he took her by the arm and guided her to the picnic site.

11

It must not be denied but that I am a plain-
dealing villain.
—SHAKESPEARE, *Much Ado About Nothing*

FOR JULIANA THE ball could not occur a moment too soon,
as she had had quite enough of this house party. Moreover,
Nicholas was studying her closely for some reason, and he
tended to appear at unexpected moments, especially whenever she sought James out. On these occasions, her husband
usually proffered a commonplace greeting and departed as
quickly as he had appeared, a practice that set Juliana's teeth
on edge.

"Whatever is he *about*, James?" Juliana asked one afternoon when Nicholas had greeted them on a particularly
isolated path in the garden.

"Why do you not simply ask him, Juliana?" James said
calmly.

"And make a cake of myself? Pray, what should I say—
'I couldn't help noticing, Nicholas, how you appear whenever I most wish to avoid you'? Only think how that would
sound!"

"Then leave off!" James said, his mouth twitching in
amusement. "You have assured me that Nicholas holds you
in no particular regard, and so if it appears that your husband

is stalking you like some prize bit of game, I can only assume we both must be imagining it. For surely we must yield to your superior knowledge of the matter."

Juliana gave him a quelling glare.

For her part Juliana found herself unable to take her eyes from Nicholas, as he was under rather unceasing assault from Lady Iphigene.

The lady peered at him enticingly over her fan, maneuvered to place herself on his arm whenever the party undertook an outing, and otherwise made herself ubiquitous. One particular episode sent Juliana into high dudgeon. It was past midnight, and the company had retired for the evening when Juliana heard a noise in the hall outside her chamber. Curious, she opened the door and peered into the hallway. Iphigene, blond hair cascading over her shoulders, was in the act of opening the door to Nicholas's room. She was wearing a diaphanous pink gown that more than adequately displayed her creamy white shoulders and certain of her other charms. Stunned, Juliana stood rooted to the spot until Iphigene disappeared through the black shadow of the doorway.

Juliana felt her heart turn over in her chest, but just as quickly the feeling was replaced by one of outrage that spurred her to action. Nicholas's chamber adjoined hers, and it was a quick matter for Juliana to locate the key and unlock the intervening door. She crept through the sitting room that separated the two bedchambers, taking up a position in the dressing alcove off Nicholas's room.

From that vantage point she saw Iphigene walk directly to Nicholas's bed and tumble onto the large sleeping form that lay there.

"Oh!" Iphigene cried out in apparent confusion as the form began to stir. "There is someone in my bed! Could it be . . . faith, I could *not* be in the wrong chamber! Oh, I have done it again!"

Nicholas's head rose from the covers, and one sleepy eye opened to behold the figure of Lady Iphigene weeping into a handkerchief.

"Oh, I am mortified beyond belief!" she said, sniffing. "Please help me!"

"As I seem to be the only one in this room to hear your cries, perhaps I can be of assistance, my lady," Nicholas said in a baritone fogged by sleep.

"Oh . . . Lord Pembroke! Why, I did not *dream* this was *your* chamber! An unfamiliar house, you know. But then it is my great burden to be plagued with the sleepwalking curse! You cannot imagine what it is like to retire to the security of one's bed and never know where one will end up!" she replied tearfully.

"Indeed." Nicholas sat up in bed and eyed the tragic figure.

"If you would be so kind as to hand me the dressing gown from the chair over there, madam, I will be happy to escort you to your rightful chamber," he said.

But at that Lady Iphigene suddenly gave a tearful cry and threw herself upon Nicholas, thrusting her arms around him and weeping helplessly onto his great chest, which Juliana saw to her horror was bare. Nicholas, in a fair way to being catapulted back into the covers, put his arms around her to prevent such a catastrophe. Juliana felt her face flame to the roots of her hair. Outraged, she emerged from her hiding place, walked over to the chair and picked up Nicholas's dressing gown.

"Were you perhaps seeking this, my lord?" she asked sweetly.

The effect of her voice on the bed's occupants was instantaneous.

Iphigene ceased her weeping and stared at Juliana in horror. Nicholas looked at his wife quizzically and allowed a slow smile to make its way across his face.

"Your timing is excellent, Juliana," he said with perfect aplomb. "Lady Iphigene was in search of someone to guide her to her chamber. Perhaps you can oblige her."

"To be sure," Juliana offered sarcastically, but Iphigene had already reached the doorway.

"So kind! But pray, do not bother! I shall manage," she said hastily, and fled.

Juliana gave the retreating figure a dubious stare and turned to leave, only to have her progress arrested by Nicholas's voice.

"I have not thanked you for my rescue," he said, studying her lazily from the bed.

"Rescue? Surely one of your size and presence needs no rescuer," Juliana replied with a skeptical arch of her brow.

"But, you see, I am in a singularly compromising position," Nicholas said, and looked pointedly at the garment that Juliana held.

She blushed and stepped over to the bed, gingerly placing the dressing gown in his hands. Quickly she moved to the door leading to her room.

"Juliana," Nicholas said.

She turned. He was eyeing her appreciatively.

"My estimation of your resources and, I might add, of your charms, grows daily," he said.

She followed his gaze and saw that it was focused on her own gown, a sheer ice-blue confection that clung revealingly to her figure. It was not her usual thing, being one of her aunt's impractical gifts, but Juliana could hardly explain that.

"Good night, my lord," she said, and hastily left the room.

Juliana found that this incident greatly disturbed her, though she was at a loss to explain why. She pondered the matter as she rode alone to Lindenwood the next afternoon to meet with the estate manager she had hired.

In truth Juliana welcomed these rides, never more than now, for they offered a solitude that helped her sort through her jumbled thoughts. The beach approach to Lindenwood was beautiful, but Juliana chose the inland trail that traversed the acres of woods between the properties because she enjoyed the contemplative mood fostered by the woodland shelter.

Why should she care whether Lady Iphigene or anyone else appropriated her husband? It was not as if the woman was stealing a march on her, for she and Nicholas did not have *that* sort of marriage. And for that Juliana was thankful. How dreadful it would be to suffer the pangs of jealousy whenever another woman batted her eyelashes in Nicholas's direction! As for Iphigene, she was no better than a common strumpet, and if Nicholas were taken with her, then he deserved all the trouble that mercenary baggage would bring him. Juliana decided it should not bother her a whit if Nicholas set Iphigene up as his mistress. Had not she been the first to suggest such an arrangement? So why did Iphigene's sneaking into Nicholas's chamber make her blood boil?

Juliana was so engrossed in her thoughts that she had failed to notice the darkening sky. A snort from Rogue brought her back to the present as the first enormous drops of rain hit her face. She pulled the horse up, realizing that if they made a break for Lindenwood, she would get thoroughly soaked. In front of them was a small path that Juliana knew led to the old gamekeeper's hut. She urged Rogue in that direction as the first bolt of thunder echoed across the sky.

She could not tell if it was the storm that made the horse uneasy, although he was not usually so skittish. Whatever the reason, Juliana had the devil of a time controlling the huge beast. They pushed deeper into the woods, threading their way through the overgrown path to the clearing Juliana knew lay only a few dozen yards before them. She had to flatten her body to the horse's neck and grab handfuls of his mane in order to keep her seat. She whispered soothing words in Rogue's ear, but he still snorted nervously.

With relief Juliana saw the tiny hut come into view. But in the precise moment she relaxed her control and sat upright, she saw what appeared to be a shrouded figure bolt out into the path. Rogue gave a startled scream and lifted his body up into the air. When he brought his forelegs crashing down, Juliana went flying over his head. A sharp pain filtered through her stunned brain, and then, mercifully, it was gone.

When she opened her eyes, she saw that she was lying before a warming fire in the small hut. Her head was throbbing.

"If you must make a habit of falling off that infernal animal, Juliana, I cannot answer for your fate. Have you thought, perchance, to find a tamer mount?"

The words made her jump, and she turned to see the hulking figure of her husband towering over her. He held a horsehair blanket, and in a moment it was draped around her shoulders. Her relief gave her voice a rough edge.

"Nonsense, Nicholas! Rogue was merely startled!" she said. After a moment she added, "I think someone must have darted into the path."

Nicholas gave her a speaking look, and she in turn eyed him suspiciously.

"I don't suppose you would have done such a thing?" she said accusingly.

Nicholas favored her with a reproachful glare.

"Such a person would have had to be either a fool or a villain," he said. "I hope that you would acquit me of both."

Juliana tilted her head as she gave the matter some thought.

"I suppose it could have been a deer," she said slowly.

Nicholas poked the fire before turning to fix her with a penetrating gaze.

"If that is how you wish to paint it, I am sure you know best," he said with irritation. "Are you quite well, by the way? Or should I say 'perfectly fine'?"

She frowned.

"You are so kind to inquire, my lord!" she said, her words heavy with sarcasm. "In truth my head seems to be the only part of me that is the worse for wear."

He looked at her, and something crossed his face, softening its sternness. He turned to the fire, pulled off a kettle, and poured a cup of tea.

"Here," he commanded gently, "drink this."

Juliana accepted the cup and took a sip. The hot liquid coursed through her body, trying to chase the chill and damp that were beginning to make her feel thoroughly miserable.

"Just how did you find me, Nicholas?" she said after a moment.

"I was out riding and sought shelter, like you," he said. "When I came upon the hut, I saw you lying on the ground and that infernal horse trying to nose you awake."

He did not mention that his heart had leapt into his throat at the sight of her seemingly lifeless body.

Juliana felt her body shiver, and she gathered the blanket around her. Instantly Nicholas was at her side.

"Are you truly well?" he asked, moving to sit next to her on the floor. The fire's glow gave his face an amber cast, and Juliana felt her heart skip a beat.

"Quite," she replied. "I was merely . . . cold."

His eyes sparkled, and a gentle smile drifted over his face.

"Perhaps I can do something about that," he said and, wrapping his arms around her, pulled her to his chest. Juliana's gasp of protest died quickly as she felt the warmth surround her and heard the pounding of his heart. For a moment the comfort of his arms blotted out the questions that simmered below the surface of her awareness and the growing feeling that some sinister something was out there waiting for her. She did not believe that the figure in the path had been Nicholas. Who was it then? And why?

Finally Juliana raised her head.

"Thank you for rescuing me, Nicholas," she said with a tentative smile.

He held her away from him and scrutinized her face. Suddenly he smiled mischievously.

" 'Twas the least I could do, Juliana, to return the favor of last night," he said.

Juliana blushed furiously. Thankfully she noted that the rain seemed to be letting up, and she put her cup aside. She could not go on to Lindenwood, in any event, as she was.

"I must go back and change out of my wet clothes," she said, averting her gaze from his.

Nicholas took her hands and helped her to her feet without a word. But when she would have turned toward the door, he refused to relinquish her hands. Slowly he brought her fingers to his mouth and caressed them with a slow, burning kiss. She stood motionless, staring. Finally he let her hands go.

"I would not want your chill to return, Juliana," he said softly, and moved aside to let her pass.

The day of the ball finally arrived, to Juliana's great relief. For it was not just Iphigene who troubled her, it was the lady's brother as well. Perceval seemed bent on turning himself into Juliana's shadow, and she would often meet him in the garden or some other out-of-the-way spot that she had sought for refuge. She found his pretentious manners and flagrant compliments a great nuisance, especially as she sensed they were as false as the rest of him. Moreover, there was something about the way he eyed her that made her uneasy.

Dressing for the ball, she sighed so often that her maid looked at her in alarm.

"Are you quite well, Your Ladyship?" she asked.

"Yes, thank you, Betty," Juliana replied, shaking her head. "I am just mightily weary of entertaining guests."

The maid looked at her mistress.

"Well, my lady, you will send them off right enough the way you look tonight," she said with an admiring smile.

Juliana stared at her reflection in the cheval glass. It was true she was in looks. She had vowed not to play the dowd tonight and had given Betty permission to work her magic.

She wore an emerald green gown shot through with threads of gold. The neckline was somewhat lower than that to which she was accustomed, displaying the creamy white of her skin and drawing the eye to her gentle curves. The clinging satin fell in a sleek line from just under her bosom to the floor, but when she walked, the fabric clung in a manner calculated to fill in many of the gaps that otherwise might be left to a gentleman's imagination. The creation admirably set off her auburn hair, which was piled loosely atop her head with an occasional wispy tendril framing her face. Nicholas had this morning presented her with an emerald necklace in honor of the occasion, and Juliana marveled at the way the candlelight caught the jewels and held their sparkle. A single emerald bob surrounded by diamonds adorned her hair.

Juliana could not have said why it was so important for her to look her best this night. She smiled to herself as she fingered the emeralds and walked to the stairway.

Nicholas, waiting at the bottom with James, looked up and drew a sharp intake of breath. James followed his gaze and then quickly returned his own to Nicholas. As Juliana descended the stairs, she was unable to look away from her husband. His black evening coat and breeches fit him to perfection, outlining his broad shoulders and sleekly muscled limbs. His shirt was simple yet elegant, and a single diamond rested in his cravat. The pewter eyes kindled with a tantalizing warmth.

Nicholas stared at Juliana, stunned by his wife's transformation into a breathtaking beauty. He took her hand and in a moment regained his tongue.

"You are very beautiful," he said finally.

"Thank you, my lord—Nicholas," she said, and smiled shyly.

Several others who studied the couple were in a rather different frame of mind. Iphigene, who stood in a corner of the room with Perceval, fairly hissed at her brother. "I shall be lucky to snare even a dance, much less get him to myself!"

"Do not worry, my dear sister," Perceval replied with a complacent grin. "If you follow my instructions, you will have your black little heart's desire!"

James had his own private thoughts as he viewed Nicholas and Juliana, but like most other matters, he kept them to himself. Still, his eyebrows knit together in a frown of concern.

After their guests arrived, Nicholas led Juliana in a lively quadrille to open the ball. A short time later, he returned to claim a husband's privilege for the first waltz.

Juliana felt a rush of delight when Nicholas clasped her waist. She looked up into his face as he drew her even closer.

"My lord, I am sure this is not at all proper!" Juliana said with a laugh.

"As we are married, do you imagine anyone will criticize our small indiscretion?" Nicholas replied with a wicked grin.

Juliana found she quite liked the warmth of that smile, and there was something about his touch that made her tingle.

"I cannot imagine anyone pressing the point against someone so . . . imposing as yourself," she replied merrily, and
caught her breath as Nicholas swirled her around in a deftly
executed turn.

"You dance beautifully," Nicholas said.

"And you, sir, are rather light on your feet as well," she
responded, her eyes sparkling.

When the music ended, Nicholas suggested a stroll in the
garden and led her onto the terrace. He drew her down a path
and to a spot from which it was not only possible to view the
sea but also to hear, faintly, its roar. He watched Juliana as she
savored the experience. The moonlight caressed her hair, and
her eyes seemed to capture the stars as she turned to him in
delight.

"Why have I not noticed this spot previously?" she said.
"For I thought to have explored every foot of this garden!"

"Perhaps we are both seeing matters in a different light
tonight," Nicholas said quietly.

Her smile faded, and her eyes grew wide as his face bent
to hers.

His mouth descended for a gentle kiss that set her heart
racing. Then the pressure of his lips slowly deepened as his
powerful arms pulled her to him. Pressed against the length
of his body, Juliana felt a queasiness in her stomach that
swelled to a wave of passion stunning in its force.

Nicholas pulled his head back to look at her face. There
was a questioning look in his eyes. With a shock Juliana
realized that every fiber of her being wanted and needed
him to continue. She touched her fingers to his face, letting
them linger on his lips.

"Please . . ." she whispered.

His mouth took hers then in a kiss that commanded her
response. Juliana found herself returning the kiss with a
sense of urgency that propelled them both into a world of
uncontrollable sensation. His mouth was assaulting hers, and

she felt his tongue push between her lips. As she pressed her body to his, Juliana heard him gasp and felt one of Nicholas's hands move to her breast. Gently he slipped off the shoulder of her gown and trailed his fingers along the creamy skin under her chemise. He bent his head to softly kiss the top of her breast. When he moved lower to touch the nipple, she cried out his name.

His head came up abruptly, revealing eyes darkened by passion and something else she could not make out.

"Have I offended you?" he asked, speaking as if with great effort.

Juliana heard his words as if through a haze, and she could not immediately find her own voice.

"No," she replied, in some confusion. "That is, I hardly know what—" She broke off. He was studying her face intently.

The moment hung between them. Juliana opened her mouth to speak.

"Lord Pembroke! Oh, I have found you at last!" Lady Iphigene's voice washed over them like a bucket of cold water.

Nicholas moved to shield Juliana while she hastily readjusted her gown, and turned toward the sound of the voice. The bushes rustled as the lady herself came into view. Nicholas sighed wearily.

"Yes, Lady Iphigene," he said in resignation. "You have indeed."

Some minutes after Iphigene had appropriated Nicholas for a dance which she said he had promised, Juliana walked alone on the terrace, trying to recover her equanimity amid the torrent of emotions sweeping through her. She was glad to be alone with her turbulent thoughts.

But she was not alone, as a pair of eyes watched her from behind a potted plant. Then the figure of the man stepped out to touch her arm.

"At last, my lady, I have found you," Perceval said, and Juliana jumped.

"I would say, rather, that you have frightened me out of my wits," she said sharply. "That is no way to accost a lady."

"And just what is the proper way to accost a lady?" Perceval said with an ugly smile on his face. "Or should I say, perhaps, a spy?"

Juliana gasped.

"What gibberish are you talking now, Sir Perceval?" she said.

"No gibberish, Lady Juliana, but the truth that I fear your husband and perhaps others of your acquaintance would be quite shocked to hear," he said.

"And just what might that be?" she said defiantly.

"Why, that the respectable Lady Juliana is one of the realm's most notorious spies and is given to dashing about the Continent in the most scandalous manner! Ah, think of the to-do! You would be quite ruined, I fear."

"You are mad!" she said, and looked frantically about the terrace.

"Oh, we are quite alone at the moment, my dear Lady Pembroke," Perceval said. "Even your giant of a husband can be of no assistance to you now, as my dearest sister has him firmly in her clutches. He is your husband, is he not? I had heard, you see, rather . . . interesting stories about the circumstances of your marriage. Perhaps you are in need of a man who can give you more than his name, my dear. Something tells me your disposition would lend itself admirably to the post of my mistress, not to put too fine a point on it."

Juliana reached out her hand to slap him, but he grabbed it and held it fast, making her gasp with pain.

"That is not the way to ingratiate yourself to me, Lady Juliana, for you must know your little game is up. I would have your favors in return for my silence, or it will be much the worst for you—and, I might add, for your brother."

Juliana cried out.

"What do you know of my brother?"

Perceval merely smiled.

"I have nothing to hide and nothing more to say to you," Juliana said firmly. "Only that I would have you remove yourself immediately from my house!"

He favored her with a mournful look.

"Since you will not listen to reason, my dear, perhaps I can offer you an alternative. While I would much prefer your embraces, I will force myself to settle for your money. Circumstances find me in need of some blunt, to be perfectly honest, and I would willingly grant my silence for the sum of, shall we say, ten thousand pounds?"

"Get out!" Juliana shouted. Perceval merely shook his head and laughed at her.

"Pity you are so stubborn," he said, and then insolently put his hand on her breast.

At that moment a couple came out onto the far end of the terrace. Juliana did not recognize them, but her relief was palpable as Perceval's face froze in irritation. Juliana seized the moment to shake off his hand and flee into the ballroom. Perceval stared after her for a moment. Then he bowed in the direction of the couple and walked off toward the garden.

Juliana did not get far before she was hailed by Lady Iphigene, who greeted her with the sort of rapture normally reserved for an encounter with some long-lost acquaintance.

"There you are, Juliana! I am particularly desirous of speaking with you," Iphigene said, bestowing a toothy grin upon her hostess.

Juliana groaned, her knees still shaking. It wanted only this.

"We are, as you may know, leaving at week's end," Iphigene began, and Juliana felt herself brighten visibly.

"But I did not wish to depart before seeing the delightful greenhouse that your husband has praised so highly."

Juliana looked at the woman in confusion. She vaguely recalled some desultory discussion about the greenhouse, but as it had been unused for years, Juliana could not see its appeal.

"I believe you misunderstood the situation, as it is in great need of a refurbishing," Juliana began. "At all events, since it was my husband who spoke about it, why, pray, do you not have him show it to you?"

Iphigene's eyes grew round, and she returned Juliana's assessing gaze with a look of utter innocence.

"Oh, I do not think that would be quite the thing," she replied. "But do say you will come show it to me now, as I am persuaded we could both use some fresh air."

"I have had about all the fresh air I can manage tonight," Juliana began, thinking that the sentiment would apply as well to the entire Smythington family. She was amazed to see Iphigene pulling her by the arm toward the terrace. "Very well, then, if you are quite determined!"

"Above all things." Iphigene smiled sweetly.

And so it was that some moments later, when Nicholas came to claim his wife for the final waltz, he did not immediately find her. Indeed, he canvassed the ballroom and then searched the terrace and the garden grounds, but discovered no trace of her.

Suddenly he heard what sounded like a shot. There was a shriek, a rustling, and then the sight of Iphigene running toward him at full tilt. She propelled herself into his arms.

"It's Juliana!" she cried. "She has been murdered!"

12

The wolves have prey'd; and look, the
gentle day, before the wheels of Phoebus,
round about dapples the drowsy east with
spots of grey. Thanks to you all, and leave us.
—SHAKESPEARE, *Much Ado About Nothing*

IT IS OFTEN true that in moments of crisis, the mind devises
its own way of bringing about that state which is most likely
to enable a person to do, in effect, what must be done.

In the instant example of Juliana, whose body had no
greater need than to summon all of its resources to expel
the foreign object, her mind—after its first great shock at the
events that had transpired—led her into a state of somnolence
that lay somewhere between hither and yon and which was
filled with the strangest dreams she had yet experienced.

She was aware of a heat in the vicinity of her shoulder;
the warmth spread to her chest, and finally her whole body.
Her mind conjured visions of Nicholas trailing kisses over
her skin, his arms crushing her in a passionate embrace that
made her body suddenly lighter—why, she was floating! She
drifted on air and found herself giggling as Nicholas reached
out to draw her back. Suddenly she felt intense pressure, and
her breast burned with a searing heat that made her cry out.
She wriggled to get free, but he held her pinioned. His body

lay atop hers, and the weight felt as if it would crush her.

"Stop! Oh, pray stop!" she shouted, and saw that Nicholas's face had begun to change before her very eyes. First it became that of Perceval, and she shuddered. Then it was James's, and she knew a moment of relief.

"Tell him, James!" she heard herself moan, even as James's face was transformed back into that of Nicholas.

But now his features bore none of the softness she remembered from his lovemaking. His blue-grey eyes glinted like steel, and his mouth was twisted into an ugly shape as it came ever closer. In her fright, she cried out. Suddenly the world grew black.

To Nicholas, the sight of Juliana lying motionless in the dirt at the greenhouse entrance gave rise to a chilling spasm of fear that momentarily paralyzed him. He heard Iphigene's hysterical babbling and was dimly aware of James carrying the woman away. His own limbs seemed to move with exaggerated slowness as—somehow—he gently lifted Juliana and, willing his body not to tremble, carried her to the house.

Later Nicholas would remember little of the next hour. The bullet had lodged perilously deep in Juliana's shoulder, and Dr. Welham—dressed in his evening clothes, for he had been among their guests—was grim as he set about the task of removing it. Juliana, drifting in and out of consciousness, cried out in pain and began to thrash about frantically.

"Hold her, my lord!" the doctor shouted, and Nicholas quickly lay his body on top of hers, holding her immobile. He thought he heard James's name on her lips, but his own brain shut out the words, and he held her fast. Trickles of perspiration ran down his face, and he closed his eyes. When he opened them again, Juliana was not moving. Nicholas's face wore a fearful question as he looked up at the doctor.

"She has fainted, my lord, and a good thing it is," that gentleman said quickly.

Nicholas gave a great sigh and felt his heart begin to beat again.

The house party, of course, was ended with no small measure of thanks due James's quickness in taking charge. Lady Iphigene, having given an account of the shooting to the authorities, was eager to stay and personally nurse Juliana back to health and to assist poor Lord Pembroke in any way she could. This plan was immediately rejected by her brother, who suddenly remembered some pressing business in London.

The grounds had been searched, but no trace of an intruder was found. Lady Iphigene had been able to recall very little of the actual events. It seemed she and Juliana had been standing by the greenhouse when the shot came from the direction of the beach. Lady Iphigene said she saw no one and, in all events, was too shaken to do naught but run for help—which, she noted, she had done instantly, despite her own considerable fear.

Lady Hereford had spent much of the aftermath of the shooting prostrate on a divan in the parlor, weeping hysterically and attended by her daughter Sarah and a vial of smelling salts. She accepted James's offer of seeing them back to Lindenwood, despite the fact that she was quite out of charity with him for not dancing with Sarah the entire evening. That his leg prevented him from doing so, she refused to acknowledge. Sarah was reluctant to leave, but James persuaded her that Juliana was being ably attended, and that at all events she would do better to help her mother.

By midday next, James alone remained at Seagate, and he waited only to ascertain Juliana's condition and assist Nicholas, whom he had not seen since his friend carried Juliana to her chamber.

A footstep at the door of the library, where James had retreated, drew his attention. Nicholas, his face looking haggard and drawn, stood there.

"I assume I have you to thank for the fact that my house has been efficiently purged of the sundry offensive personages who have occupied it these too many days," Nicholas said. He carried two glasses of brandy and handed one to James.

James accepted the glass and searched Nicholas's face.

"Juliana?"

"She will live," Nicholas said. "At least that is what Dr. Welham believes. But she is not out of danger, yet. She must be watched closely for fever and infection."

James's shoulders relaxed in relief.

"I have the utmost confidence in Juliana's constitution, Nicholas," he said calmly, drinking deeply.

Nicholas eased into a chair and likewise took a drink. One hand absentmindedly rubbed his chin.

"I believe you have known Juliana a long time, James?" The words were delivered quietly, but James's antennae instantly were alert to a sense of danger.

"Since before her father's death," he responded.

"Do you know anyone who might wish to do her ill?"

James ran his finger along the top of the glass.

"I do not know why Juliana was shot, Nicholas," he said, after a moment. "I do, however, intend to find out."

"As do I, James. As do I," Nicholas said quietly.

Nicholas rose from his chair and walked to the window where he stood watching some gulls squabble over their luncheon. The day bore an eerie stillness that bespoke a coming storm, and indeed the clouds had already begun to roll in from the sea. Devoid of the sunlight that usually streamed in the windows, the library wore a dark and somber air. Finally Nicholas spoke.

"I am grateful, my friend, for your assistance last evening, and I collect you have been a friend to Juliana as well as myself," he said. "But something here is amiss, something beyond the tragedy of last night. If you can by your actions help Juliana, I will be eternally grateful.

"But," he continued, his brow furrowed as if in deep concentration, "if you have in any way contributed to her troubles, I will not answer for your fate."

Nicholas's voice held not a trace of malice, but James felt rather than heard the threat. He returned Nicholas's measuring glance with one of his own. Then each man downed what remained in his glass and rose to leave.

Juliana opened her eyes and saw with relief the familiar blue canopy that topped her comfortable bed. What nightmares she had had!

But just as quickly her relief gave way to dismay, for a dull pain was emanating from her shoulder, and she found that when she tried to move, it was not so easily accomplished. She attempted to sit up and instead gave a cry of pain. Instantly she saw the form of her husband before her.

"I do not believe, Juliana, that you are in any condition just yet to attempt such a task on your own. Allow me to help you," Nicholas said, and reached his powerful arms under her body to raise her gingerly into a sitting position. He took some cushions and positioned them behind her back.

Juliana was silent throughout this process, trying to sift through the confusion in her brain. She closed her eyes, and images floated before her—Iphigene, the greenhouse, Nicholas. Abruptly she opened them.

"I was shot," she said.

"Yes."

"Do you know who did it?" she asked.

"No."

Juliana closed her eyes. Nicholas sat down on the edge of the bed and took one of her hands in his.

"You have been out for several days, I'm afraid," he said kindly, "but you are safe now."

She lay back in the bed and surveyed her husband. He looked positively ghastly. His clothes were disheveled and seemed as though they had been slept in. His lined face was that of a man ten years older. His bloodshot eyes looked at her with concern, and she found herself wanting to reach out and smooth his rumpled hair. Then she surveyed her own situation and flushed in embarrassment. For—how could she not have detected it immediately?—under the covers she had on not a stitch!

"Might I trouble you for a dressing gown?" she said, her mortification giving her complexion an unusually reddish glow.

Nicholas looked about him helplessly.

"The wardrobe, there," Juliana said, pointing.

He opened the door she indicated but was confounded by the baffling array of garments. He smiled wryly.

"I will send your maid to you," he said, and pulled the bell. "If there is nothing else you require, madam, I will leave you."

Juliana shook her head, and he moved to leave.

"Nicholas," she said.

He halted at the threshold.

"Yes?"

"Did you, ah . . . tend to me, all this time?" she asked hesitantly.

"But of course," he said with a mischievous grin. "You were in the best of hands."

13

I may chance have some odd quirks and
remnants of wit broken on me, because I
have railed so long against marriage: but
doth not the appetite alter?
—SHAKESPEARE, *Much Ado About Nothing*

"THIS IS NONSENSE, Nicholas! Put me down, pray! 'Tis my shoulder that is injured, not my legs!"

Juliana grimaced in exasperation as her husband, ignoring her protests, carried her down the stairs and out onto the terrace. He placed her gently in a chair and pulled another one up beside her. A chess set was laid out on a nearby table, and Juliana saw several books and a swatch of her needlework.

"There. I thought we would pass the morning in the fresh air," Nicholas said. With a wave of his hand he gestured to the items. "You have only to ask, my lady, and whatever amusement you wish shall be handed to you on a silver salver."

Juliana laughed in spite of herself.

"Nicholas, this is ridiculous! I am perfectly capable of managing. You need not play nursemaid to me, you know," she protested.

"Alas, the lady would deprive me of her company, and just when I thought we had passed a thoroughly enjoyable sennight!" Nicholas responded mournfully.

"Enjoyable? Perhaps if one is fond of being confined to one's bed! Really, Nicholas, it is time I manage on my own now. I do not need your help to do *everything*!"

Although, Juliana reflected, she had rarely enjoyed a week more, despite the unfortunate fact of her injury. Nicholas had gone to great lengths to see that she wanted for naught. He had been constantly in attendance, entertaining her by reading aloud or trying to best her at chess (although she always gave a good accounting of herself). Sometimes they simply talked, and for Juliana this was the most pleasurable of all. For the first time since they had known each other, she found herself entirely at ease in his presence.

Dr. Welham now came only on alternate days, and on the other days Nicholas insisted on checking her bandage himself, to Juliana's embarrassment. She had not forgotten the passionate interlude they had shared on the night of the ball, and the intimacy of his touch made her blush. But, she reflected, there was nothing of the lover in the way he efficiently checked her dressing or carried her about. On the contrary, his was the demeanor of one whose interest in the patient was that of a concerned brother.

Juliana sighed. She supposed she should be grateful for that. This new easy companionship allowed them to spend time together comfortably, without the sparks that had ignited on previous occasions. After all, she reminded herself, wasn't friendship what she had sought for this temporary marriage?

"Well, my lady, and what is your pleasure? Chess? A book, perhaps? I have here Mr. Defoe's inestimable yarn, which I think might appeal to your sense of adventure," Nicholas was saying.

"You mean my sense of isolation, don't you, Nicholas?" Juliana replied. "For you have me shut up here as if I were shipwrecked on some desert island. And you are a far more demanding companion than Mr. Crusoe's Friday!"

Nicholas gave her a wounded look.

"You have read it, then? And here I thought to delight you with a diverting tale!"

"I read it when I was nigh still in leading strings. My father was most insistent that his children learn about the world beyond their immediate experience," Juliana replied.

"Is that why he schooled you in the classics? In my experience it is unusual for ladies to know a Greek chorus from the tabbies that preside at Almack's—come to think of it, perhaps there is not much difference," Nicholas said with a broad grin.

Juliana's eyes twinkled appreciatively.

"But if you had studied your Horace, you would know that is the case," she said. "*Coelum non animum mutant qui trans mare currunt.*"

Nicholas gave a delighted smile.

" 'Those who cross the sea change climate, but not their state of mind,' " he translated. "To be sure, Horace had the right of it. But tell me, Juliana, why did you never join the throngs of misses who made their pilgrimage to that worthy institution in search of a husband?"

Juliana was taken aback at his abrupt shift of subject.

"Why, you know my circumstance, sir!" she said in surprise. "My parents' deaths made a Season impossible."

"Perhaps at the beginning, but surely you could have pursued it after your period of mourning ended," Nicholas persisted gently.

Juliana was silent. A gentle breeze blew across the terrace, and she sat back in her chair to let it soothe her.

"Marriage is not a state that I prized over-much, sir," she said finally. "It would seem to be the occasion of restricting one's choices rather than expanding them."

"And yet that is the way of our Society for women such as yourself," Nicholas said with a smile. "Do you think, then,

Juliana, that men are such brutes that no amount of affection can tame them into civilized companions for one's advanced years?"

"I do not think about affection," she said grimly. "It is treacherous to allow one's emotions to dictate the circumstances of one's life. That produces only the worst sort of pain and folly."

" '*Coelum ipsum petimus stultitia,*' " Nicholas quoted. " 'In our folly we seek the very heavens.' "

Juliana's head jerked up angrily.

"You mock me, my lord," she said.

"Nay, Juliana," he said, placing his arm gently on hers, "for I know too well passion's folly. It does not follow, however, that passion is ever treacherous, that love will always betray. For that is how you see the loss of your parents, is it not—as a betrayal? But it was not their love that betrayed you, surely."

Juliana covered her face with her hands.

"Not their love, sir, but mine!" she cried. "Had I not loved them so well, perhaps I would not have felt the loss so deeply. I could not bear to lose anything so dear ever again!"

Nicholas reached out his hand and stroked her hair soothingly.

"And yet it is not sorrow you feel, but anger. Why is that?"

Juliana's head came up abruptly. Tears streaked her face.

"My parents' death was no accident, Nicholas. They were murdered, surely as I sit here, by Napoleon. My father was a good and decent man who believed in serving his country, despite his wealth and a title that ensured he would never have to lift a finger to do more than summon his servants. But he served his king, and he died for it!"

She gave a gasp of horror. She had not meant to share this pain, but the words were already out. Moreover, she knew she could not unburden herself of the worst of it.

With overwhelming despair, she buried her face in the handkerchief Nicholas held out. Her shoulders shook as she sobbed. After a time, she blew her nose and looked over at him in embarrassment.

"I did not mean to turn into a watering pot," she said with a tentative smile through her tears. "Pray, accept my apology."

Nicholas smiled gently and picked up a book. "I do believe you have never heard Mr. Defoe to better advantage than when he is delivered in my own dulcet tones."

And he began to read.

Juliana was most insistent several days later that it was time she rode again. She was already dressed in her riding habit when she greeted Nicholas at breakfast and announced her plan to reacquaint herself with Rogue.

Nicholas studied the set of his wife's jaw and abandoned the idea of dissuading her from such a foolhardy adventure. But, as he told her sternly, she would go nowhere without his escort, and they would, in any event, attempt only a short excursion.

Moments later, Nicholas found himself fighting back doubts as he surveyed Juliana's horse and watched his wife transported into raptures at the gigantic animal's snort of welcome.

"Dear Rogue, I have missed you these weeks! Oh, Peters, say you have not neglected him, for he looks so eager to be off!"

"Nay, Miss Juliana, me and that cursed animal been out most every day working out the fidgets in 'im. Otherwise, 'twould not be fit for riding!" was the groom's dour response.

As if he disagreed with Peters' assessment, Rogue shook his giant head and bellowed a protest.

Nicholas looked at the beast skeptically. He was a huge gelding with a gleaming black coat, and his eyes shone excitedly at the sight of his mistress but with a wildness Nicholas could not like. Nicholas counted himself an excellent horseman, but he would not care to ride the animal in his present mood. He was quite certain he did not wish Juliana to attempt it.

"Juliana, perhaps this first time a gentler mount would be more the thing," he said, gesturing at a stall further down. "There is Bluebell, for example—a sweeter temper you would never find, and yet she has spirit."

"Oh, Nicholas! As if I would think of riding aught but my Rogue today!" she said. "Come, or I shall leave you behind!"

They set off at a moderate pace, with Peters following closely behind them in the event, as the groom said in a comment that further unsettled Nicholas, my lady found herself with more horse than bottom. Not, Peters quickly added at Juliana's thunderous look, that she couldn't handle her Rogue.

Nicholas soon found his fears somewhat allayed, as Juliana's firm hand restrained the animal with only a little difficulty. After a quarter hour, however, Nicholas observed that her face was pale and her lips were pressed together tightly.

"Are you well, Juliana?" he asked in concern.

" 'Tis just the effort of maintaining such an awkward pose," she said. "Though I had never noticed it before, sitting the sidesaddle forces my shoulder into a position it seems to prefer to avoid, at least under the present circumstances."

Nicholas saw that her injured shoulder, twisting forward slightly to compensate for the angle into which the sidesaddle forced her lower body, looked deuced uncomfortable.

"Clearly you are not yet ready to ride, Juliana. Let us head back and resume this activity when you are better," Nicholas said.

He was surprised when Juliana turned her mount around without a protest, but he soon found that was not the end of it. The next morning, she appeared at breakfast in a pair of breeches.

"I mean to ride today, Nicholas, and not a word from you will persuade me against it!" she said defiantly. "I have found more suitable attire, you see, and need not sit the sidesaddle."

And so it was that Nicholas, against his better judgment, found himself accompanying his wife as she rode astride the beast, apparently in perfect harmony with the creature. At one point, Juliana gave a delighted shriek and spurred Rogue to a wicked gallop. Nicholas rode after her in alarm, but he pulled his horse up short when he saw that she had stopped at a tree to wait for him with a mischievous grin.

"You cannot think to catch me, Nicholas! For, I'll wager Rogue and I can beat you to that hedgerow yonder with no difficulty!"

Nicholas looked at his wife in exasperation.

"I did not allow you to ride so that you would end up with worse injury than before," he said sternly. "You must pace yourself, Juliana, and stop taking such foolish risks."

She looked over at him with a haughty elevation of her brow, but there was a twinkle in her green eyes.

"Did I understand you to say, my lord, that I needed your *permission* to ride? Well, it is time you learned that Rogue and I intend to do just as we please!"

With that she spurred her mount, who was all too willing, and dashed off in the direction of the hedgerow.

Nicholas gave a snort of exasperation, but it faded into a smile as he watched Juliana lead her horse in an all-out romp across the field. A stream of sunlight caught the highlights in her auburn hair, and he heard the tinkling of her laughter. She sat the animal so perfectly that he knew with certainty she had done so all her life. Her hips and thighs, outlined with such shocking distinction in those breeches she wore, were positioned tantalizingly above her mount. Her legs clung so snugly to the beast that Nicholas inadvertently found himself imagining them wrapped about him in a rather different sort of exercise.

Abruptly he shook his head in amazement and, spurring his horse, started after her.

The days of August found those of September but gave neither Juliana nor Nicholas reason to interrupt their pleasant idyll, for that indeed is what it had become.

Days were often spent on horseback, as Juliana delighted in showing Nicholas the countryside that surrounded her beloved Lindenwood and which had provided a cornucopia of delightful adventures when she was a child. They walked down to the beach, and once Juliana shocked Nicholas by proposing a swim.

"My dear Juliana, it seems appropriate to note the obvious—that we have not the proper attire for such an adventure," he pointed out.

"Pah! If Robert and I had let *that* stop us when we were children, I daresay we never would have so much as wet our toes!" She laughed scornfully.

Her eyes sparkled, and her brows arched a challenge.

"Are you really so stuffy as all that, Nicholas?" she asked with a mischievous grin.

She saw that his own mouth was beginning to twitch, but his next words made her blush.

"No, Juliana," he replied calmly, his eyes meeting hers with an altogether different sort of challenge. "But do try and remember that I am neither a child nor your brother."

She found herself tongue-tied and looked away in embarrassment. On the horizon she saw some fluffy clouds gathering in the distance.

"I daresay it may blow up at any moment, so perhaps we should forget the notion," she said hastily.

"I daresay," he replied, and Juliana was sure she heard repressed laughter in his voice.

Afternoons found them on the terrace, reading or playing chess, often interrupting these pursuits to engage in spirited but friendly argument.

"Some would say that Mr. Crusoe was extremely adept at using his wits. Others attribute his good fortune and survival to the intervention of divine providence," Nicholas said one afternoon. "What say you, Juliana?"

Juliana tilted her head in a gesture Nicholas was coming to know quite well as she pondered the question.

"I think that while there is no question providence put into Mr. Crusoe's hands the means by which to survive, he was an extraordinarily *resourceful* man," Juliana said.

"Yet his life had not fared particularly well previous to the disaster that landed him on the island," Nicholas persisted. "Why had he not used his resources until then?"

"I suppose one does not know fully the extent of one's abilities until tested in ways not previously anticipated," she replied after a moment. "When the question is one of survival, I suppose a person does what he must."

Nicholas frowned as he noticed for the first time the position of Juliana's rook. He was silent for so long that Juliana was surprised at his next words.

"And how do you think you would have fared in his stead, Juliana? Do you think your resources would stand such a test?" he said as he eased his queen out of harm's way.

Juliana thought for a moment, for she had come to know Nicholas well enough by now to realize that he was in earnest. It was often his scholar's habit to take a subject and move the conversation with his questions into new and surprising directions.

"Well, although I have lived by the sea most of my life, I do not have Mr. Crusoe's knowledge of the sea. By that I mean the kind of knowledge of the currents, ship's supplies, carpentry and the like that served him so well at the start," she said. "And of course women are not so strong as men. But as to the latter question, well, I do consider myself somewhat resourceful, Nicholas, and I like to think I might have come about."

Nicholas did not respond immediately, as he was attempting to recall where else he had heard his wife praised as "resourceful." An image of Sir Perceval came to mind, but that left him even more puzzled. He forced his concentration to the game at hand.

"I see, madam, that I have underestimated your resourcefulness in at least one endeavor. For your next move would seem to be to capture my queen with your own."

Juliana gave him a mischievous smile and promptly complied.

And so the time passed in pleasant fashion. Nicholas occasionally took an hour during the afternoon to work in his study, but he was often surprised to observe that he had little inclination for the task.

By tacit agreement, they did not discuss the shooting, nor indeed did there appear to be any development on that front. Nicholas himself had mounted a thorough search of the grounds and found no clue as to Juliana's assailant, nor did he find any signs that the intruder remained about. Likewise, there had been no word from James. And so the silence over this particular event provided each of the parties with a welcome opportunity to put it for a time from their minds in the interest of pursuing more placid and, indeed, healing endeavors.

Juliana found herself drawn out of her customary reticence about her person and into wide discourse with Nicholas about her childhood, travels with her parents, and the loneliness she experienced in the years after their deaths.

"Are you ever lonely, Nicholas?" she said to him one afternoon.

He thought for a moment.

"I suppose scholarship is a lonely field," he said. "As a youth, I was sometimes isolated by my love of learning at a time when many of my fellows were enjoying more frivolous pursuits. But I never regretted my choice. And now, although of necessity I do my work alone, I would not say that I am lonely."

Juliana listened to him gravely.

"Perhaps that is one of the differences between us, Nicholas. For there are times when I feel a great loneliness. Although," she added thoughtfully, "there are fewer of those times now."

And it was true, she acknowledged. She was thoroughly enjoying Nicholas's companionship as well as their rides, their walks, and their discussions. Never had she had such a friend, and that was what he had become. That was, of course, as well it should be, given their arrangement. But there were times, Juliana acknowledged, when the fact of his friendship left her . . . unsatisfied. There was something else she wanted, though try as she might, she could not—or would not—name it.

Alone at night in her room, Juliana thought of the man in the chamber next to hers and felt her face grow warm. She saw the image of Nicholas lounging sleepily in his bed, his chest bare, the night she had routed Iphigene. She remembered the power of his arms during her convalescence when he had literally carried her everywhere. And of course she could never banish the sensation of that kiss they had shared in the garden. The friendship they shared was pleasant, she mused, but it lacked the passion of those earlier moments. Then she smiled in chagrin. Passion. Was that what she missed? Surely not!

Juliana pulled the covers up to her nose. What was it that Nicholas had written? "Some individuals . . . have higher susceptibility to passion's sway. . . ." What did that mean, really? She trembled, but whether in fear or anticipation, she could not have said.

In the adjoining chamber, Nicholas was having similar thoughts. Though he was careful to adopt with his wife a demeanor of placid friendship, he had found himself thinking increasingly about her in a way that was more than friendly. He did not know when that had begun, although he distinctly remembered the warmth she had generated in him on a number of occasions—her saucy ride on that infernal creature, her daring suggestion that they strip to their essentials and swim that day on the beach. And, although his concern over her injury had always been uppermost in his mind in the days when he tended her, he had not been blind to the beauty of her body. As for that night in the garden, he had tried to put the memory into the more distant recesses of his mind, but it continued to intrude with irritating insistence. He had been within moments of taking her then and there, their guests be damned! Nicholas groaned. This was not precisely the marriage he had bargained for.

And so the halcyon weeks passed with both parties engaged in mutually rewarding and civilized friendship by day, but each undertaking a tortured self-examination by night that resulted in a state of perplexity, consternation and, above all, dissatisfaction.

14

> You are more intemperate in your blood
> than Venus, or those pamper'd animals that
> rage in savage sensuality.
> —SHAKESPEARE, *Much Ado About Nothing*

THE UNEASINESS THAT intruded into this otherwise blissful interlude finally recalled both Juliana and Nicholas to their senses.

Nicholas, who had temporarily abandoned the search for his mysterious spy, decided it would be more fruitful to divert his frustrations to that endeavor than to allow thoughts of his wife to keep him awake at night.

Juliana, judging herself fully recovered, sent word to James that she was mindful of her duty and more than ready to resume her work. Indeed, there was ever more need for such services in the unfolding drama. Napoleon had driven the Allies out of Dresden, but his army had been diminished in the process and was plagued by supply problems and low morale. It was believed by some in the English government that the emperor now had no choice but to retreat and abandon the Elbe, but others—James among them—sensed that Napoleon was not yet done for and was planning a great battle to save his empire while there was still time.

In London, James fingered Juliana's letter. Virtually all of his agents were working to ferret out the emperor's next move. In all likelihood, Juliana could contribute little that was not already being done. He knew that he should refuse to allow her to continue to jeopardize her own life, but his eye strayed to his desk, on which lay a coded communication from Robert. He was their most important weapon now. And he would head straight for Juliana.

There was really no choice. James sighed and fervently hoped Nicholas never discovered what he was about to do.

As they usually took tea in the garden in fair weather, Nicholas was perplexed at Juliana's absence. Nor did she seem to be anywhere at Seagate, he discovered in a quick search of their usual spots. When he summoned his butler to inquire, that impassive emissary brought him a note in Juliana's hand.

"As I have longed to see Elise these many weeks, pray do not be overset that I took it in my head at the last moment to dash off to visit her. I expect to be away for several days. Juliana."

Nicholas frowned uneasily. He had not forgotten the state in which she had returned from her last visit with Mrs. Duville. Moreover, he did not like her about when the circumstances of the shooting were still unsolved. Finally he was forced to acknowledge that the house seemed quite empty without her presence. He was, in fact, at pains to find sufficient activities to distract him for the remainder of the day. He spent the next day in his study working and tending to correspondence, but thoughts of Juliana kept intruding. By the third day, he decided more productive pursuits were called for.

Suddenly his face lit up. He would ride to Mrs. Duville's and surprise Juliana. He supposed it was not quite the thing for a husband to sit in his wife's pocket, but he found that he wished to see her above all things. His spirits cheered instantly with the thought.

The cottage was just as he remembered it, and Nicholas walked confidently to the door. There was no immediate response to his knock, although he thought he heard a slight shuffling on the other side of the door. Finally it opened slightly, and the gnome-like face of Elise Duville peered out at him. She gave a cry and slammed the door.

"Madam! It is Lord Pembroke! Pray, open the door. You cannot think I mean you harm!" Nicholas said in perplexed amusement.

The door slowly opened, and the woman peered up at his great height.

"And what, *m'sieur*, may I do for you?" she said with a frown.

"Why, I am here to see Juliana," Nicholas said amiably. "Surely you do not mean to forbid me the company of my own wife!"

Mrs. Duville blanched.

"I am afraid, my lord, that Juliana is not here . . . at present," she said.

Nicholas frowned.

"Not here? Then she is away at the moment? I should be pleased if you will suffer me to wait for her return," he said.

She shrugged.

"You may stay for a bit if you must," she said uncharitably.

Nicholas accepted her offer of tea and sat down to wait. An hour passed, and he found himself shifting about impatiently. Mrs. Duville had long since given up the effort of making conversation and was sewing in the corner, eyeing him occasionally.

Finally Nicholas could bear the inactivity no more.

"Madam, if you would please inform me as to where Juliana has gone, I shall seek her there."

The woman returned her sewing to its basket and fixed Nicholas with a direct, unblinking gaze.

"My lord, I cannot say."

Nicholas was hard-pressed to stifle his irritation.

"Pray, what do you mean, madam?" he said impatiently. "That you do not know where she is, or that you do know and are not at liberty to reveal it?"

Mrs. Duville looked up at him, clearly unhappy. She did not approve of Juliana's dangerous activities. Perhaps, somehow, this giant of a man could put a stop to them. She shrugged.

"I do not at this moment know where Juliana is," she said at last. "Although I am not certain that if I did know, I would tell you. Juliana has been my charge since she was a babe, and I cannot betray her. But neither will I lie to you, my lord. She is not here and has not been for nigh onto two days."

Nicholas stared at the woman open-mouthed, and then his face began a slow burn that seemed likely to end in the emission of smoke from his ears had he not turned on his heel and taken French leave.

For Nicholas, the words could only confirm his worst suspicions, the nagging thoughts that had lain dormant during these idyllic weeks after festering in some layer of his brain that had chosen to keep them buried and silent.

His wife had a lover.

Riding home, Nicholas pondered this notion. The enigmatic subject of the man Juliana professed to love had not been broached since the argument shortly after their wedding. Juliana had seemed happy enough these last weeks, and Nicholas supposed he had assumed that whatever infatuation plagued her had disappeared.

He laughed bitterly to himself, and his brow furrowed with fury. So she had, all the while, yearned for another. During their desultory walks, their stimulating discussions, their exhilarating rides, she had secretly pined for someone else.

Who?

The answer came to him with simple clarity, an echo of his secret fears.

James.

He spurred his horse on.

Juliana waited for the door to open. She was so exhausted, she could barely stand. She and Peters had ridden straight from the inn at Tunbridge Wells, where she had spent the morning with James discussing what they both hoped would be her last trip to France. She took a deep breath and prayed that this time they would meet with success.

She had agreed to meet James halfway from London after his urgent message requesting the meeting. But she had had to wait at the inn one futile day while James was delayed in town. She and Peters had ridden most of the afternoon and evening to get back, with those cursed hills south of Mayfield slowing them dreadfully.

Juliana supposed she looked like the devil. She wondered what Nicholas had thought of her absence and smiled at the prospect of seeing him again.

In his darkened study, Nicholas was a portrait of brooding gloom. His cravat had long since been discarded, and his shirt was open halfway down his chest. He propped his long legs carelessly on the desk as he leaned back in his chair and stared at the carved ceiling. An empty glass rested lightly between the thumb and forefinger of one hand, and a half-empty decanter stood open on the table near his chair.

It had taken all his power of will not to ride directly to London and confront James. At the last moment he had realized bitterly that James likely was somewhere else making love to Juliana.

Nicholas's thoughts were a jumble of anger and frustration even as he sought to make sense of this madness. On the one hand, he could scarcely blame Juliana for what she had tried

to confess from the start. Their arrangement, after all, allowed
neither of them a claim on the other's heart. But she had lied
about visiting Mrs. Duville—this time and probably on that
earlier occasion—and thus had violated her promise to behave
with honor. And it was more than that, Nicholas thought as he
refilled his glass and drank deeply. He felt betrayed, deeply
and personally betrayed, by the fact of her having taken a
lover. The anger and hurt threatened to consume him.

A sound in the hall drew his attention. He looked at the
clock. It was nearly eleven. He found his feet and quietly
opened the door. On the stairway ahead he saw the bedraggled figure of his wife as she made her way up the stairs.
She looked extremely tired, and he knew a moment of blind
rage when he contemplated what could have left her in such
a state. He set his glass on a nearby bookcase. Soundlessly
he moved to follow her.

Juliana had not rung for her maid, deciding it would be
quicker to undress herself and simply fall into bed. She
removed the pins from her hair and brushed it as it fell,
creating an auburn halo about her shoulders illuminated by
only a single candle. She discarded her dress on the chair
and stood there wearily, clad only in her chemise. Suddenly
she heard a creak. She stared in amazement as the door of
her chamber swung open.

Nicholas stood at the threshold, and Juliana gasped in
shock at his disheveled appearance. His shirt was open
nearly to his waist, exposing a swath of curly dark hair
on his chest. Her eyes moved up to his face, and what she
saw there sent chills down her spine. His dark brows were
knit together in a brooding scowl, and his eyes were hard and
cynical. He looked down at her from his great height with
a distaste that twisted his mouth into an ugly expression of
scorn. He stepped into the room and, without a word, closed
the door.

Juliana looked at him uneasily.

"Nicholas, you do not appear to be quite yourself tonight," she ventured cautiously.

"Whereas you, my dear, are thoroughly yourself at last," he said menacingly.

She paled.

He reached out and with his fingertip touched the lace that edged the neckline of her chemise. She did not move.

"Is this what you wore for James?"

Juliana gasped.

"How did you know about James?" she asked in a hoarse, amazed whisper.

Nicholas smiled grimly, shaking his head at her confirmation of his suspicions.

"I think perhaps it is I who should be asking the questions, Juliana. Did you think to play me for the fool with your lies? Did you think I would never learn the truth?"

"I had hoped to have it over and done, and to spare you the necessity of finding out," she said, looking down at the floor.

Nicholas stared at her in angry confusion.

"So it is ending, then?"

"There is to be one last time," she said. "I cannot refuse."

She raised her head defiantly.

"I *will* not refuse, Nicholas. It is everything to me. You cannot stop me," she declared, as her heart pounded in her ears.

Nicholas, whose control had been hanging by a thread, felt his anger explode in the face of her brazen challenge. He grabbed her hair and roughly forced her head back.

"Oh, I will not stop you, my dear. But I will make it so you will never lie with another man but that you think of me," he said, and brought his lips down on hers with bruising force.

Juliana tried to cry out, but his lips held her prisoner. He pulled her body to his, nearly crushing the breath out of her.

She felt his hands move over her hips, pressing them to his, and then begin to roam her body.

She felt the length of him against her and tried to push him away. But she was helpless against his force. Abruptly Nicholas scooped her into his arms and carried her to the bed. He threw her down roughly, and she gave a gasp of terror.

"Nicholas!" she cried, but broke off when she saw him cast off his shirt. As she stared in wordless horror, he sat down on the bed and removed his boots. Then he turned to her, grasped her chemise and ripped it down the center. She screamed. He quickly removed his breeches and moved his body over hers.

He brought his mouth down on her lips with a force that sent her senses reeling, despite her fear. She closed her eyes, and tears silently rolled down her face. Nicholas felt the moisture and lifted his head. She held herself rigid as he studied her features and then, abruptly, thrust himself from her.

"I cannot," he said quietly. "Though you be the worst sort of slut imaginable, God help me, I cannot."

Juliana looked at him in shock. Then she reached up and slapped his face with all her strength.

"I hate you!" she shouted and, turning away from him, buried her head in her hands and broke into great sobs.

Nicholas stared at her as she huddled naked on the mattress, her body heaving, her back to him. He found himself shaking. He had gone against his nature and was appalled by the fact of it. Whatever she had done, he had not the right to violate her, and it shook him to the very core to see how close he had come to it. For despite his size, indeed perhaps because of it, he had never taken advantage of another's weakness.

The room was silent, except for the sound of Juliana's wrenching sobs and the frightful thunder of his own heartbeat. The moment stretched into an eternity.

Finally, without a word, he lay down and reached his long arm across her, gently cradling her body in his as she wept. They lay thus for a long while, until Juliana's cries were spent.

After a time Juliana became aware of the body that held her close and the arm that enveloped her in a great, gentle bear hug. The warmth generated by this presence comforted and soothed her, and she no longer sensed the anger that had been there. No, here was the quiet spirit, the friend she had come to trust. She reached out to touch the hand that covered hers. It pulled back, as if startled. Then it returned, gingerly, as if fearful of frightening her with its great power.

They lay there in a silence that was complete, yet deafening in the communion of their two spent spirits. Juliana began to stroke the hand with her delicate fingers and, without knowing why, reached out and brought it to her lips. She heard a sharp intake of breath from behind her, and then felt the warmth on her neck as the air was expelled. The body behind her seemed suddenly rigid, as if afraid to move. Juliana reached her hand back to draw it nearer. They lay together, spoon fashion, and Juliana knew a moment of profound contentment.

Then somehow her body was wriggling almost imperceptibly against his—as if, Juliana thought in wonderment, it had a mind of its own. The great arm pulled her even closer, and she became aware, suddenly, of an overwhelming force that had replaced the gentle warmth. Juliana felt herself in its grip and was surprised to find that she had no wish to be otherwise. Inexorably, she felt herself turning around, and then she was suddenly looking into a stricken pair of deep, blue-grey eyes.

"Nicholas," she whispered. "Oh, Nicholas!"

He said nothing but studied her face, his own expression grave. She reached a tentative hand up to touch his cheek and was startled when he caught her wrist. Gently he kissed her palm, and she felt her pulse quicken. His mouth moved down to her wrist and then to the delicate white of her arm as she willed him not to stop. When he did stop, she opened her mouth in a protest that was quickly silenced by a kiss so soft, so deliciously sweet, it made her tremulous body ache with desire.

Suddenly she was impatient with his gentleness, and her own mouth responded with fire. She kissed him with an urgency that demanded an echo and quickly found it. Their lips became bruising instruments of passion as each sought the other with a hunger that knew no bounds.

With a great effort Nicholas finally ended the kiss and raised his head to look at her. He took in her flushed complexion, her swollen mouth, and the luminous green of her eyes.

"Juliana?"

He had spoken so softly she could scarcely hear the word. But she heard the question and knew the answer. She reached out and drew him down to her.

Their bodies moved together in a symphony of understanding, each sensing the other's need. Nicholas, marveling at the softness of her skin, rained kisses over the whole of it as Juliana trembled in delight. Her feather-light fingers toyed with his hair and sought to memorize the planes of his face and the hard muscles of his arms and chest. They clung together, seeking the ultimate closeness until, finally, Nicholas joined his body to hers. Juliana gave a gasp of pain, but her mind refused it, and she was quickly caught up in the rhythm of his movement and intimate caresses. They held each other fast until uncontrollable waves of pleasure engulfed them both.

The room grew silent, and Juliana lay contentedly in Nicholas's arms. Her breathing fell into the gentle rhythm of sleep. Nicholas studied her peaceful smile, somehow incongruous with the tear stains that even now remained on her face.

But he was not at peace. At their moment of most profound pleasure, his captive heart had been wrenched from him, catapulted into a guilty hell of his own making. He was horrified, stricken unto death by this night.

His wife had been a virgin.

15

When you depart from me, sorrow abides,
and happiness takes his leave.
—SHAKESPEARE, *Much Ado About Nothing*

JULIANA STRETCHED OUT her toes, her hand lazily reaching across the mattress as her mind hovered between sleep and waking. She was searching for something, wondering in her haze what it was. Suddenly she knew: it was the warmth, the gentle warmth.

But her hand found only a cold, empty bed. Her eyes flew open. The sunlight streamed in through the window, but she saw only images from the night: Nicholas's face just before he kissed her, the blue-grey eyes glowing with passion, his powerful body as it shared its secrets with her. Reluctantly she forced her eyes to focus on the room, and they instantly spied the note on the mantel. Even before she read it, she knew he had gone.

"My dear Juliana," it began. "My deepest apologies for what violence I have done you, as well as for the insult of impugning your honor and offending your sensibilities. I will always regret my mistake. I have absented myself in order to complete some unfinished business. It is my hope that this will also allow both of us time to recover some measure of equanimity. You have my vow that I will henceforth uphold the terms of our marriage agreement. Nicholas."

Juliana crushed the note and threw it against the wall. Mistake! So that is how he thought of their lovemaking! Juliana angrily punched the mattress. Nicholas thought he could remove himself and all would be as before. She shook her head. Perhaps that was a suitable remedy for him, but it was too late for her. Her eyes lingered on the crumpled note. She walked over to where it lay, picked it up, and smoothed it out.

"Nicholas," she whispered softly, and clutched the paper to her breast.

It sometimes happens that the significance of momentous events is not always immediately apparent. While there are those who instantly recognize them as such and know their lives to be forever altered, others fail to judge such moments correctly, perhaps because their natures are less able to penetrate straight to the heart of the matter, so to speak. One might think that Nicholas, with his demonstrated abilities at that clarity of thought needed for such scholarship as he daily pursued, might be of the former persuasion and that Juliana, whose life was daily marked by the need for duplicity and secrecy, might be of the latter.

Nay, for human nature often does confound even those most practiced at its observation. Juliana, who despite the turmoil that her secret life and submerged passions had inflicted on her soul, knew instantly that her night with Nicholas had forever changed her life. Although she had heretofore determined to keep passion at arm's length, as it were (and indeed, had successfully carried out that philosophy), the experience of embracing it at last had the effect of removing blinders from her eyes. She discovered how well-founded was her fear of love because she saw with devastating clarity the perilous state of vulnerability in which she now existed. At the same time, she knew her soul immeasurably enriched by that love and understood that she could never, would never, wish it otherwise. That she remained, for the moment, without the object of that love did not alter her opinion.

For Nicholas, however, it was another matter. He did not doubt that his night with Juliana was of grave import, but he failed to see, precisely, its true impact. He was so overcome by regret at his own behavior, by shock at discovering his wife innocent of those apparent crimes of which he had blindly formed a certainty, and by something else that acted, literally, to propel him from her bed. That something was the strong, clear image—appearing in his mind as he lay next to Juliana—of the presence that had sent him to Sussex in the first instance. The image was of a worldly but somehow vulnerable tavernmaid who had in a few short hours captured his heart and who, until those placid days spent with Juliana, had fully occupied his thoughts. Just why such a vision had appeared in the very aftermath of such sweeping passion with Juliana disturbed him greatly. For he saw with additional horror that he had further wronged Juliana by taking the gift of her body and, in essence, defiling it with the image of another.

So it was that Nicholas's gift for penetrating the myriad philosophic treatises and deepest obscurities of humanity failed him in the instance of his own situation. His eye was clouded by remorse, by guilt, and especially by an obsession of which he knew he must rid himself before he could even look at his wife again with straight-faced sincerity. That he was swept away by the feelings and sensations of the night, in a way that had never occurred previously, he noted but failed to fully examine, as is the way sometimes of men.

And so he rode like a madman through the villages along the coast, plying fishermen with gold and trying to loosen the tongues that could free him.

•   •   •

"It must be today, Juliana," James was saying, as Juliana forced her mind to abandon, for the tenth time, the question of where Nicholas might be and how long he intended to remain. It had been nearly a week since he had gone.

"What, James? I am sorry, I must have been wool-gathering. Something about today?" she replied distantly.

James rose angrily from the chair he occupied in the morning room at Seagate and walked over to place a hand on Juliana's shoulder. He shook it roughly.

"Juliana, heed me well. I do not know what has put your brain in a fog, but if you do not rid yourself of it, this mission will be gravely imperiled!"

Juliana shook her head to dispel the unbidden images that had surrounded her.

"Nonsense, James," she said briskly, rising. "I am perfectly fine. Pray continue."

"I said that you must leave for France today. We expect word from Robert hourly. That he has left Paris can only mean one thing: Napoleon has made his decision."

Juliana felt her heart rise to her throat. Nevertheless, her words were calm.

"I am ready, James. I shall summon Peters."

It was late afternoon by the time the three of them arrived at Mrs. Duville's. The steep pathway afforded swift and direct passage down the cliff to the secluded cove where the schooner awaited. The captain and mate were in James's employ, it being the latter's customary responsibility to assist Juliana at Ambleteuse and row her back to the boat. They were efficient, experienced men, and neither James nor Juliana had had occasion to worry about Juliana's safety. Only the dour but vigilant Peters had ever protested the arrangement. He had not liked to remain behind on shore awaiting his mistress's return. But Juliana, knowing Peters would never be mistaken for a Frenchman, had always insisted that it was necessary for him to serve as the cove's watchman and to have horses at the ready. Nevertheless, he always watched her departure with a scowl.

He was scowling now as James handed Juliana into the fishing boat. At the last moment James reached out to embrace her.

"Have a care, Juliana!" he whispered urgently.

Nicholas was beside himself. All his inquiries had led him to the same place. His thoughts were a morass as he stood before the wooden door, trying to make sense of the odd looks and veiled hints he had received these past days. It seemed that the existence of mysterious nighttime goings-on around Pevensey were well known to the villagers hereabout. Mostly they involved smuggling and the like, and Nicholas quickly learned that his sympathies for such operations (along with a few pieces of gold) were essential to pry information from the taciturn and distrustful lot who fished these waters. He had learned about lace stuffed into geese and hams, brandy kegs concealed in lobster pots, and packing cases marked "returned Government stores." When he gave them to understand he was not interested in free trade so much as he was in a certain red-haired miss who might occasionally travel the channel by schooner, the guidance he was given had been the same that he had received so many weeks ago from Jonathan Greeley.

And so, as he knocked impatiently on the door, he wondered just what new obfuscation Mrs. Duville would have for him now.

The door opened, and two beady eyes peered up from the tiny face. Nicholas expected her to shut the door on him, but instead she opened it wide. Her eyes were red, and her face bore a worried look.

"My lord," she said with an inquisitive note in her voice. She waited for him to state his business.

"Madam, I know we have spoken of this matter previously,

but I have reason to believe that you can direct me to a certain Frenchwoman I have been seeking these many weeks. Before you deny me, let me say that unless I find this woman, I cannot answer for my fate, or indeed that of my wife. For I have wronged Juliana, of that there can be no doubt, but I find myself unable to redress these wrongs unless I have laid to rest my obsession for the other. I only know that I must find her and that somehow she is tied up with any hope I might have of making Juliana happy. Nay, but my very soul desires to see her face."

He took a deep breath and waited.

Elise Duville stared up into the lined face that bore the tortured look of a man at the end of his resources. She said nothing for a moment, as impulse warred with her fears. Finally she made her decision.

"I cannot help you find your mystery woman," she said, as Nicholas's spirits plummeted. "That you must do for yourself. But," she continued, "if you have a care for your wife, she is at the beach down below at this very moment jeopardizing her life."

Nicholas stared. Then he abruptly turned and ran from the cottage.

The last glimmer of the sun's fading rays illuminated the horizon as Nicholas gained the beach from the rocky pathway. The tide was in, and the uneven strip of sand was narrowed to a ribbon when he paused at the base of the cliff. He could just make out the silhouettes ahead at what appeared to be a small dock. One of the figures was a woman he guessed to be Juliana. She stood against the sunset and embraced one of the men as he handed her into the boat. When the man turned, exposing his countenance to the faded orange light, Nicholas recognized him as James.

Clambering over the rocks, Nicholas maneuvered his way closer. The boat was pulling away, and he saw the woman turn and wave briefly to James. Nicholas was close enough to see that she was dressed in a ragged, wrinkled frock that looked as if it belonged to a scullery maid. The uneven light cast her smudged face into the shadows, and her hair hung down in disarray. Nicholas knew, though he could not see for certain, that it would be auburn, even as he knew her eyes would be green. His heart raced in anticipation. He had found her. He started forward as she turned her face to the light. What he saw made him gasp in shock, although one tiny corner of his mind told him he had known all along.

Nicholas was not the only one who found the boat's departure a matter of great interest. Sir Perceval Smythington smiled from the rock outcropping into which he had tucked himself in order to determine to his own satisfaction that all was going as planned. And, he thought with silent glee, all *was* indeed going well. True, there had been some . . . false starts. By rights they should both have perished in that carriage accident, and the high and mighty Lady Juliana might well have come to her reward in the forest or at the ball. But then they would not have had this dramatic climax to events. He had been able to keep track of her movements through the mercenary offices of one of the workmen involved in the refurbishing and later by bribing one of the stablemen. As for that brother of hers, Perceval's connections in France had decided to wait until Robert made his move. Give him enough rope, so to speak. Perceval frowned. He did not like to fail. And this time he would not. Quickly he slunk away in the shadows.

By the time Nicholas reached the dock, the schooner was in deeper waters, and only James and Peters were left on the shore. Peters saw him first, and his mouth gaped open. But James remained staring at the receding figure, preoccupied by an unaccountable sense of danger he could not shake.

Suddenly a chilling voice from behind startled him from his reverie.

"Tell me, James," Nicholas said quietly, "how long has my wife been a spy?"

16

I do much wonder that one man, seeing
how much another man is a fool when he
dedicates his behaviours to love, will . . .
become the argument of his own scorn by
falling in love.
—SHAKESPEARE, *Much Ado About Nothing*

SOMETHING WAS AMISS. Juliana was as certain of that as she
was of her own name. She thought it devilish queer when
that odd-looking ruffian on the boat offered a Banbury story
to explain the absence of the regular mate. Although the
captain vouched for the new man, Juliana's senses began
to tingle a warning. She did not like having to depend on
a stranger at such a time and thought it odd James would
not have mentioned the change.

No, Juliana thought, there was definitely something
smoky about it all. She had left the new mate at the shore
and ridden to the tavern on a horse she hired from a village
connection whose silence was customarily purchased as well.
But the nag that he offered this time was a broken-down piper
who looked as though he was not even fit for the merest child!
She had eyed the man skeptically when he professed to have
no others in his stable.

Now, as she studied the ancient oaken door, her nerves

were on edge. The crowd in the tavern consisted of the usual thatch-gallows and assorted villains, and their company afforded her no great peace of mind. Juliana had long perfected the veneer that allowed her to shrug off their coarse comments with a careless smile; at all events, Michele always saw to it that she was rarely alone in the taproom. But only the knowledge that this would be the last time allowed her to endure it now. Whenever the door opened, she fought against an impulse to jump. Just as well, she thought, that most of the louts were too occupied with their brew to notice her odd behavior.

It grew late. The roar of revelry engendered by the various spirits had long since given way to an unsavory air as several of the patrons sought to top off their libations in amorous pursuit of the various chambermaids eager to augment their small wages in such manner as they could. Juliana knew she was courting their fate, and indeed Michele had frantically been motioning her to the sanctuary of his family's quarters this half hour. But she ignored him. Despite her misgivings, her instincts of danger, and the sordid scene in which she now found herself a reluctant player, Juliana was powerless to leave. She knew there would be no second chance. She took a deep breath. She had not come this far to turn hen-hearted.

When the figure appeared, she was not prepared for the panic that coursed through her entire being. He was gaunt, and his face bore the look of one with the devil at his heels. He was wrapped in a black cloak that stood in stark contrast to the pallor of his complexion. His eyes looked out of sunken hollows, and he walked barely ten feet into the room before collapsing at her feet.

"Robert!" she said, and gasped.

Her cry was lost in the din, but one or two fellows eyed the newcomer with interest. Juliana quickly recovered. Gesturing to Michele, she smiled archly.

"Pah! This one has had too much to drink! And I suppose

he wants a place to sleep off his head. Help me prop him up here, dear cousin, and we shall see if he has a sou to his name!"

They sat him in a chair in the corner, and Juliana knew a moment of sheer terror when she wondered how she would manage to get her brother home by herself.

"What he needs is an undertaker!" came a slurred shout from the corner, and the room erupted in laughter. Juliana forced a smile onto her face, but her heart was quaking. That he was injured likely meant there was someone in close pursuit.

"Michele!" she whispered. "Help me get him to the stables!"

The Frenchman was happy to oblige, as he had quickly ascertained that it would be best to rid his doorstep of this dangerous package. Juliana draped one of Robert's arms around her shoulders, and Michele took the other. Together they managed to carry Robert out the door, the unceremonious escort of an unconscious inebriate barely noticed in the revelry. But as they emerged into the stableyard, a horse thundered to a halt in front of them. Aghast, Juliana looked up in fear.

Staring down at her from a great height atop his mount was her husband. His raven hair had been blown into wild disarray by the wind, and his pewter eyes glinted with an air of torment that gave his lined face the look of one possessed.

"Nicholas!" Juliana cried.

He returned her stare with an assessing gaze of his own, but he made no move to dismount. Instead, his eyes coldly studied Robert as she struggled under the burden of his dead weight.

"Please . . . !" she urged. "We must get him out of sight. There is no time to lose!"

He took in the plea in her face and the raw emotion in her voice. There was a moment of hesitation. Then he was on his feet, carrying Robert to the stables and placing him down on some straw.

Robert moaned, and Juliana rushed to lay her face against his chest. She mopped his brow with the hem of her dress.

"Dearest! We shall soon have you safe!" she said, her voice catching in her throat.

He stirred then and, opening his eyes, beheld his sister's countenance.

"Juliana, my love!" he began, but closed his eyes in pain and could not continue.

"Don't speak! We will have you safe soon enough," she cried, pressing him gently down.

But he moved her hands away and struggled to speak.

"Leipzig . . . It is Leipzig," he rasped. "Two hundred thousand strong, not enough . . ."

His lips moved again, but Juliana could not hear the words. She bent forward to put her ear near his mouth.

"The fourteenth . . . 'Tis to be the fourteenth," he whispered. With that, he collapsed back onto the straw, his chest shaking from his efforts.

Juliana felt his weakened pulse. She placed her hand on his chest and found to her horror that it was covered with blood. She turned to Nicholas, her eyes pleading.

"Please help me save his life! We must get him back to England!"

Nicholas heard only the roaring of his own pulse as he dispassionately surveyed the man who possessed Juliana's heart. A voice, it might have been his own, calmly whispered in his ear and told him what a fool he had been. All the time she had pined for this poor devil and risked her life for this man she called "dearest" in a way she had never addressed him. Her affections were returned, of course, for had not the man called her his "love"? The voice laughed at his folly, and Nicholas felt as if his very heart had broken into tiny pieces. His spirit sagged with the knowledge that there was no longer hope. He had found his mystery woman and his wife, and lost them both in one night.

But as he looked into her stricken face, he knew he could not refuse her. Quickly he reached over to check the man's wound and saw that the makeshift bandage covering it was soaked with blood. He turned to Juliana, his pain giving his voice a hoarse, ragged sound.

"Give me a piece of your petticoat, my dear," he said roughly, "that is, if you wear one under that infernal rag!"

Juliana quickly tore a piece of fabric and handed it to him. She watched, her hands trembling, as Nicholas applied pressure to Robert's wound and efficiently wrapped the fabric around the soaked bandage.

"This should be cleaned and bound anew, but we do not have time. Come!"

Nicholas and Michele hauled Robert up onto Nicholas's horse. Nicholas mounted and put his massive arms around Robert as he grabbed the reins.

"Juliana! I thought you said there was no time to lose!" Nicholas said harshly, and with no more urging she scrambled to her nag.

Their pace was slowed by Nicholas's burden and by the reluctance of Juliana's mount. The wind whipped up, and Nicholas fought an unbidden image of that first night when they had made a similar dash to safety. He shook his head and recalled his mind to the present.

Now, as he looked at the figure of his wife astride that godforsaken nag, he saw that she was bent over the animal's neck, coaxing him, willing him to move as if the hounds from hell were on their trail. Nicholas smiled sadly. She still rode like an angel.

Juliana clasped her brother's limp hand and adjusted a pillow that cushioned his head. He lay on a bunk on Nicholas's yacht, which sailed toward England as swiftly

as wind and tide permitted. Her spirits warred between worry
over her brother's condition and anger at how they had been
betrayed.

There had been no mate waiting to row them, no fishing
boat waiting offshore. They had been abandoned to their
fate. Or at least, she corrected, they would have been, had
Nicholas not come to their rescue. Juliana closed her eyes.
How had Nicholas come to follow them across the channel?
He had saved their lives. And now he knew all. They had
not talked about it; indeed, they had exchanged few words
this night. Was he angered by her deception? Their only
encounter on board had occurred when he stopped into the
cabin briefly to check on his passengers. He inquired politely
about her own condition and was gone. She had not seen
him since. At least, she thought, now there would be no
more deception. Things could be different between them—
she only prayed it was not too late.

On deck Nicholas pondered the depths of the swells that
rose and fell with a rhythm that lulled his brain into a
numbness that unfortunately was all too temporary a state.
It was a choppy ride, but he supposed the man in his cabin
did not feel the roughness of their journey. Would he live?
Nicholas shrugged. His death could not affect his own future,
for Nicholas saw his marriage for the charade it had been.
Juliana had wed him because it preserved her opportunity to
work for this man's freedom. And now she had succeeded.
Only an annulment stood in her way, and Nicholas knew he
must allow that to go forward.

It was that thought that sent his spirit to the bottom of
the sea. Lord Pembroke at last had witnessed the blinders
fly from his eyes, and they lay in shattered pieces about
his feet. Nicholas now knew with blinding clarity and the
immutable certainty that comes with life's great moments of
truth that he was finally, irrevocably, in love with his wife.

17

~~~~~~❦~~~~~~

For which of my good parts did you first
suffer love for me?
Suffer love,—a good epithet!
I do suffer love indeed,
for I loved thee against my will.
—SHAKESPEARE, *Much Ado About Nothing*

THE EVENTS OF the next few days moved so swiftly that
Juliana scarcely knew how she kept her head from spinning.
James met them at the dock with a prisoner in the person
of one Sir Perceval Smythington, whose unctuous smile
was noticeably absent. Dr. Welham attended Robert and
pronounced that while his wound was grave, he was
likely to live. James hastily returned to London with
the information Robert had nearly perished in delivering.
Nicholas was nowhere to be found, having vanished after
helping deposit Robert at Seagate.

Gradually Juliana's mind began to absorb the pieces
of the drama as she spent the hours in her brother's
chamber, tending his wound and exchanging stories of their
adventures.

"Only think, Robert!" Juliana said one afternoon as she
and her brother were engaged in a game of chess. "That
snake Perceval was in the employ of the French all along!

And to think he passed above a fortnight in this very house with that horrid sister of his. A more insulting, odious man I have never encountered."

"It was more than insult, Juliana," Robert said, his brows knitted together in concern. "It seems he had been plotting your demise these many months."

Juliana looked at him, still finding it hard to believe that he was restored to her. His face yet bore a sickly pallor, but he was on the mend, and for that she would be eternally thankful.

"And yours, brother dear. Or had you forgotten?" she said with a frown.

Robert smiled wanly.

"I am not likely to forget that night, Juliana, as you know. Had those two ruffians not jumped me as I was fleeing Paris, I would not still be imposing on your hospitality. Your presence is, as always, delightful, but I would dearly love to be in London now, plotting anew with James."

"Ruffians! Nay, and you know they were not, Robert! Napoleon's men, I'll warrant. We know they were but waiting for you to make your move!" Juliana persisted. "Perceval indicated as much the night of the ball."

Juliana paused, her thoughts on that harrowing moment in which her brother had entered the tavern. She had been sure he was mortally wounded, a thought she had never shared with Robert. Still, he was improving daily, thank God. If convalescence could keep him out of James's schemes for a little longer, the Corsican would be done for, and there would be no need for Robert to cast himself further into harm's way. She threw her hand up in a sweeping motion of dismissal.

"As to that, it seems Perceval's competence was no better than his honor," she said. "I cannot think there was aught to give us much worry after all."

Robert caught her hand in his, forcing her to meet his eyes.

"I cannot like your casual dismissal of his perfidy," he said in exasperation.

Juliana suppressed a smile. Ever ready with a challenge, he was recovering his spirit nicely.

"Oh, not his *perfidy*, surely! It is simply that he did not *succeed* in it, you know. I am, after all, perfectly well. And while you, frankly, have appeared to better advantage, I believe you shall be up and about, breaking the hearts of breathless young ladies in no time at all." Juliana studied the chessboard. "It does seem as you have my rook cornered."

"Juliana."

She looked up mischievously. Robert was so serious that it was tempting to tease him, although she knew this was not really a joking matter. He studied her in frustration.

"That traitorous devil was responsible for the broken axle that almost sent you and Nicholas to your deaths, not to mention the bullet that ended up in your pretty shoulder!" Robert expostulated. "He planted the saboteur on the schooner who forced the captain at pistol point to abandon us to our fate! That you and I survived can be attributed more to providence, and to the considerable efforts of your husband, than to any incompetence on Smythington's part!"

Juliana flushed at his reference to Nicholas, and Robert saw in dismay that tears had suddenly appeared in her eyes. He gave her hand a reassuring squeeze. She responded with a tenuous smile and forced her attention to return to the game.

Juliana had to pace her brother's sickroom for six days before any word came as to Nicholas's whereabouts. A letter arrived one afternoon as Robert lay napping, and she immediately settled into a corner of his room to read it.

Juliana, the letter began, *I am in residence at my estate in Yorkshire . . .*

"Yorkshire!" Juliana shouted in chagrin. Startled out of his sleep, Robert opened his eyes and beheld the flushed countenance of his sister, who had risen from the chair and was clutching the epistle with a look of confused consternation.

. . . and expect to remain here for some time. I think it best to cede the field to your young man . . .

"My young man?" Juliana said wonderingly.

. . . whom I have no doubt you have nursed back to health by now.

"Robert! He means you!" she cried as that worthy pulled himself up in bed and stared. "But 'young'? Why, you could give me two years!"

"Juliana, whatever are you screeching about?" he asked grumpily.

"It is Nicholas," she replied, waving the letter in his direction. "He is rusticating in Yorkshire!"

"That is indeed alarming. To have one's husband disappear into such a wilderness . . ."

Juliana jumped to her feet and began to pace as she read aloud:

" 'I daresay I cannot stand this godforsaken country for three years . . . ' "

"Three years!" Robert ejaculated. "The man must be mad!"

" ' . . . but I shall at least leave you in as much peace as is in my power. Regrettably, that night of love we shared . . . ' "

"Night of love?" Her brother directed an interested gaze at Juliana.

"Never you mind! The rest is private," Juliana said, and abruptly fled for the sanctuary of her own chamber.

" ' . . . that night of love we shared has complicated our arrangement, but I fully intend to make it up to you," the letter continued. "You shall be free to marry the man you love."

"Foolish man!" Juliana cried.

She jumped to her feet and crossed the chamber, turned, and walked back again. This continued for some minutes. Still she could not think of what course to take, short of ordering the carriage immediately for the journey to Yorkshire.

"And why do you not do so?" Robert asked later when she was wringing her hands in frustration before him. "Or write him at least? It is such a silly misunderstanding, after all. All you need do is tell him I am your brother, goose!"

" 'Tis not that simple, Robert. I believe he has seized upon your existence as an excuse to avoid me altogether! He never wanted our marriage in the first instance. He thinks me a dowdy nobody and cannot wait to be rid of me!"

"What about the 'night of love'?" Robert asked pointedly.

Juliana flushed.

"I believe Nicholas was not at all himself that night," she said haltingly. "At all events, I am sure he must despise me. After all, he knows that my life has been one great lie! How can he not wish me at the bottom of the sea?"

"Well, and perhaps he does not, sister dear. All of your protestations do not answer why you cannot simply write him a letter explaining this misunderstanding," Robert insisted.

"If he knows that he has mistaken you, he will feel that he has wronged me," Juliana said quietly. "I do not want guilt to bring him to my side, Robert."

Robert looked at his sister. Her lower lip trembled as she fought back tears.

"After all your impassioned diatribes over the years about the folly of love," he said gently, "I suppose I should be surprised to find you so in its clutches.

"But," he added after a moment, "I am not. For you have always had a loving spirit, Juliana, and I am happy that you have discovered it at last."

He reached out his arm and patted her hair.

"You and Nicholas will come about, dearest," he said reassuringly, "for how could any man resist such a prize?"

Juliana threw herself into his arms.

"Oh, Robert. You were always on my side, were you not?"

"And you on mine, Juliana," he replied with affection, "as you have proven these many months by risking your life in a way I cannot like but which I have every reason to be thankful for."

He held her away from him and studied her face gravely. "Juliana, promise me you will do no more work for James. For I do not wish such a life for my sister, and I cannot think that Nicholas would want such for his wife."

She smiled through her tears.

"I promise!"

Robert recovered enough to remove to Lindenwood, which was empty at last of Lady Hereford and her daughter, as they were enjoying the delights of the Little Season. Indeed, Juliana's aunt had besieged her with invitations to join them in town, knowing that the daughter of a marquess who was also the wife of an earl could only add to the considerable approbation and countenance which were, to be sure, due Sarah in her own right. Still Lady Hereford liked to hedge her bets and was most insistent that Juliana comply.

Juliana surprised everyone by agreeing to go to London when Robert declared himself ready to return to work at the Foreign Office. She declined to join Lady Hereford and Sarah at her uncle's townhouse, however, nor would she move into Robert's. Rather, she settled into Nicholas's abode on Brook Street in the event he should somehow take it into his head to travel to London.

It was during the third week in October that Nicholas did indeed find himself in his carriage bound for London. It was not merely that he could no longer abide the remoteness of Yorkshire, although that was certainly true; he could no longer concentrate on his studies as he had in the past. It was not that he was leagues away from any of his usual habitats, although that was also true. And it was not that he was tired of his own company, although there was absolutely no doubt of that.

Simply put, Nicholas had discovered he could not endure an existence without Juliana. He found he had no taste, after all, for the empty nobleness of his gesture. Stepping aside to facilitate her happiness with another had seemed like the proper thing to do for one's beloved, and the honorable course under the circumstances. But it did not fill the aching void in his heart. And it did not warm his bed at night. No, Nicholas had found that after years of secluding himself in his study and his scholarship, years of avoiding conflict in the interest of congenial congress with humanity, he had—at long last— a wish to join the fray.

He had decided to fight to keep his wife. Was there any chance she might return his affection? As he thought about the night they had shared, he recalled moments in which he did not think she was altogether indifferent to him. And if she were not indifferent, Nicholas thought he had the advantage over his competition. After all, Juliana was his wife, and there were certain . . . advantages that state offered to one determined on a course of passionate persuasion.

He watched the Essex countryside slip past his window. He would love to bring Juliana here, but today he was not even tempted to stop. Indeed, he was filled with anticipation as he contemplated seeing James this very afternoon. The shock of discovering his wife to be a spy had faded into the realization of how little he knew of the woman he married. That would change, Nicholas thought grimly. He wanted every shred of information about Juliana that James had. He would know her, and he would win her.

Nicholas stretched out his feet on the opposite seat and summoned the image now never very far from his mind's eye. It was of an auburn-haired woman with a maddening habit of pacing a room when her mind was actively pursuing a dilemma. Her Latin was excellent, her Greek only fair, but she was a passing good chess player, better at whist, and superb at sitting a prime goer. She had a way of pondering a question by tilting her head and then delivering her thoughts with stunning directness. She was all too accustomed to hiding her charms in a variety of shapeless gowns that Nicholas vowed would be the first to go.

He smiled. When had that image supplanted the one of his exotic French spy? He thought perhaps it had happened a long time ago.

"Robert! I do have a mind to pay a call on James to see if he has word of Nicholas," Juliana said as she swept into her brother's study at Linden House on Charles Street.

"My dear, if anyone has word of Nicholas, I do not see why it would not be you," Robert said, but he smiled as he observed his sister.

Juliana could not have been lovelier in her Devonshire brown velvet walking dress that looked as though it had stepped from the pages of *La Belle Assemblée*. The reddish-brown tint highlighted her auburn tresses, which were only partially covered by a matching cossack hat with peacock feathers on one side. Soft tendrils had been allowed their freedom in order to frame her face, from which a pair of emerald eyes gleamed with excitement. The effect was breathtaking, and Robert rose to greet her with a kiss.

"Juliana, you look quite the beautiful lady about town today," he said. "I wish you were here to play hostess, as I know it would do me the veriest credit."

Juliana smiled wistfully and gave him a gentle nudge.

"Robert, you know I must remain at Nicholas's house while there is any hope of luring him from the wilds of Yorkshire!"

Robert eyed her with interest.

"Do I detect, perhaps, a plan forming in that beautiful head of yours?"

Juliana returned his gaze with bland innocence, but in truth, she had thought of little else during her stay in London. To her surprise, she had found the endless parties and diversions of town entertaining. They had, after all, filled the time. But they had not served to alleviate the dull ache and constant longing that plagued her through the days and far into the night. She had no trouble pinpointing the focus of her yearning. He had mesmerizing pewter eyes, a towering presence, and massive arms that could be wondrously gentle. He was irritatingly persistent when his mind was set on a subject. His maddening remoteness could suddenly give way to an engaging smile that made her heart flutter. His nature tended toward congeniality, but Juliana knew it belied a volatile passion simmering beneath the surface. She felt her skin tingle at the thought of just how deep that passion ran. Her face grew warm, and she felt the familiar rise of impatience that had gripped her since she had begun waiting for Nicholas to return to her.

As Juliana's was not a passive nature, it had not taken long for impatience to win the day. She was tired of the waiting game. Surely she was not so impoverished of resources that she could not manage to get one man to journey two hundred miles to London! No doubt it would take cunning, she acknowledged, for she had vowed not to put the matter to him directly. And so, when deviousness was called for, Juliana had decided to turn to one whose practice in that skill made it a form of art.

"I thought to put it to James, you know, the task of drawing him to town," she told Robert in a sudden rush of words. "I cannot ask Nicholas myself, but I think perhaps if James could get him here and we were to meet, I could show him that I am not an utter dowd and . . . perhaps persuade him that remaining married to me could be, well . . . acceptable."

"And just how would you propose to do that?" Robert asked. "Not that anyone with a particle of sense wouldn't leap at the chance to have you at his side!"

Juliana blushed. Marriage did have *some* advantages, after all, but she could not bring herself to discuss that with her brother. She shook her head.

"That is my own affair," she said and, picking up her reticule, moved briskly to the door. "Come, brother dear, I have need of your escort. We are going to see James!"

18

I was not born under a rhyming planet, nor
can I woo in festival terms.
—SHAKESPEARE, *Much Ado About Nothing*

ALL IN ALL, he was well satisfied with the way events
had turned out, James thought. A slight frown wrinkled his
brow. Well, not completely satisfied—there were a few loose
ends. But as a close observer of human nature, James had
confidence that certain misguided parties would eventually
resolve their difficulties. While those very parties were at
that moment heading in his direction, James sat compla-
cently in his study pouring himself a glass of Madeira to
celebrate the momentous news he had just received. He
was in the very act of reflecting that it would add to his
enjoyment were there one with whom he could share this
pleasure, when a knock on his door preceded his butler, who
intoned Nicholas's name.

"Well met, Nicholas, indeed!" James said as he rose to
greet his friend, and then caught sight of Nicholas's somber
face. "Do not tell me you intend one of your harangues, for
my spirits are far too high today."

"Harangues? Never say so, James!" Nicholas responded
gravely, although James discerned a mischievous light in
the blue-grey eyes. "Although if you will continue to ill

use those of us foolish enough to call you friend, it is only reasonable that you meet your share of disapprobation from time to time."

James offered Nicholas a glass of Madeira and gestured to a chair.

"I see you have not forgiven me, Nicholas, for not being completely truthful about . . . matters of state," James said, eyeing his friend.

"Matters of state be hanged, James," Nicholas rejoined quietly. "It is the matter of my wife that concerns me."

James pulled out his handkerchief and began to polish his quizzing glass. For once he opted for a direct approach.

"I suspect you blame me for Juliana's involvement in this murky business," he said. "Nevertheless, you have not been married to the lady for these months without learning that she has a mind of her own."

Nicholas fixed him with a hard look.

"My dear James, Juliana was engaged in work that was not only dangerous in itself, it was doubly so because she was largely left to her own devices. I profess myself mightily dissatisfied with the arrangements you made to safeguard her life, all of which were easily penetrated by one dastardly villain!"

James studied the quizzing glass, held it to his eye and, apparently satisfied with the results of his labors, let it drop.

"In that, Nicholas, you may be said to have a point, although I assure you it was not for want of intent to protect her," James said. "You know I would not willingly risk any life, much less Juliana's."

"What I know about you, James, gives me no great confidence of that at all," Nicholas replied scornfully. "For in the matter of scruples, the difference between you and Sir Perceval is largely one of address and the fact that you are on our side."

James did not take offense at this remark, nor could he when he knew the truth of it. Moreover, his spirits were too buoyed to allow them to be dampened by logic or accusation. He clapped Nicholas on the back.

"Come, Nicholas! I know you did not journey here to chide me on my character," he said. "For unless I miss my mark, you have other matters to discuss."

Moving to the mantelpiece, he added casually, "Just how goes the fair Juliana, my friend?"

Nicholas gave him a speaking look.

"James, you must know I have not seen my wife since the night I expended considerable energy rescuing that young pup who claims her heart!"

"Young pup?" James eyed Nicholas in puzzlement.

Nicholas rose and found that he had the strongest inclination to pace the room, a realization that made him wince.

"Let us not mince words, James," Nicholas began. "I told you that our marriage was not . . . the usual thing."

Here, he did begin to pace in earnest. Finally he stopped in the center of the room in exasperation.

"Juliana told me at the outset she cared for someone else and had obligations that necessitated my assurance of her independence. We agreed to seek an annulment after a suitable period. Then things . . . changed. At first I believed she had a lover, and I was ridiculous enough to suspect you of playing the part," Nicholas said.

There was a choking sound, and Nicholas looked up to see James pounding vigorously on his chest as he tried to recover.

"Yes, I know it was absurd." Nicholas grinned wickedly. "You are not really Juliana's type after all."

James glared indignantly, but Nicholas continued.

"I know now, of course, what those obligations were— to her country and to your dastardly operation. I learned in France who was the object of her affections."

Comprehension was beginning to dawn on James's face, but he remained silent.

"Needless to say, James, none of this would be trouble-some had I not come to lose my . . . indifference toward my wife. I had thought, in a noble sort of manner, to vanish with my studies in Yorkshire and leave the way clear for Juliana to be with . . . her gentleman. But I found that such altruism, though it may have suited those blasted philosophers with whom I have spent most of my life, did not suit me at all."

Nicholas took a swallow of his Madeira.

"I do not know how things stand between Juliana and me, James," Nicholas said, "but I intend to find out. And I desire your complete honesty, that is, as much as you understand the word. To wit, James, how did Juliana get drawn into your insidious net? Be frank. I wish to know what drove her so eagerly into danger's embrace."

James fixed his friend with a quelling look. After a moment he gave a great sigh and walked over to his desk. Taking out a small miniature, he handed it to Nicholas.

"This was William Westlake, the previous Marquess of Linden, Juliana's father," James said. "He was perhaps the cleverest agent this office has had occasion to employ. He was daring, quite handsome as you can see, devoted to his country, and as conversant with the French as anyone not of that nationality."

Nicholas studied the figure. He was drawn instantly to the piercing green eyes, now disturbingly familiar.

"Lord Linden was my mentor, like a father to me," James said, looking at a point slightly above Nicholas's head. "I learned a great deal from him and was often at his home. Juliana and her brother were as my own family."

A wistful smile flitted across his face and then was gone.

"There was only one area in which Linden's enemies could find him vulnerable, and that was his family. He was devoted to them, and everyone knew it."

James's fists clenched, but it was the only sign of emotion he betrayed.

"I fancy that after Linden hatched the scheme that devastated the Danish fleet, Napoleon was seized by an apoplectic desire for a particularly vicious sort of retaliation. For we have reason to believe that the target of that carriage accident was to be Lady Linden and the children."

"But the children were not with Lord and Lady Linden at the time," Nicholas said.

"No. They had stayed behind in London with Lord and Lady Hereford," James said. "William and Madeleine acceded at the last hour to Juliana's request that she and Robert remain with their aunt and uncle in order to see the horses at Astley's. And so they did. Linden took the children's place in the carriage so that he might escort his wife to Lindenwood. You know what happened."

Nicholas fingered the miniature.

"Juliana was, of course, devastated over the loss of both of her parents, but especially aware that it was because of her that her father was in the carriage. I believe she wished for a time that she had perished in his stead, but it was not long before she turned her grief into action and came to me with the plan by which she and Robert would continue with their father's work."

James took the miniature that Nicholas held out to him and returned it to his desk drawer.

"I did not think it would go this far, you see. At first their work involved only innocuous trips to Paris, where Madeleine's family lived, and bringing back what tidbits of information they picked up. Both Robert and Juliana speak the French of their mother, you see—to be sure, I would not have entertained the notion if there were any chance they could be perceived as British!"

Nicholas took another sip of wine and allowed a slight elevation of his brow.

"Certainly not," he said dubiously.

"Then Robert volunteered to infiltrate the Corsican's command, as he had a cousin who served the emperor and who would vouch for him. I agreed, never thinking he would be successful. But he began sending us useful information. Juliana volunteered to act as courier, as she had a trusted acquaintance who allowed her the use of his inn near Ambleteuse, a ramshackle sort of place that is quite a haven for all sorts of—but I forget myself. You have seen it, of course."

Nicholas's face was unreadable, and James continued.

"I thought not to involve her in such dangerous duty, but she is quite a resourceful agent, Nicholas—and an excellent shot and horsewoman, by the way. There was no doubt she had the skills for the work. So I agreed. You would have done the same thing, I'll warrant."

"Oh, no doubt," Nicholas said sarcastically. "Why should men have all the fun in war? It is high time that the ladies make themselves useful. I do not know why I had not thought of it previously. Why, they are an excellent source of cannon fodder!"

James gave him a wounded look.

Nicholas placed his glass on the desk and turned to take his leave.

"I have heard enough, James. I believe I know the rest of the story. What I don't know is how Juliana came to fall in love with one of your agents, and I do not think I care to hear that."

James threw up his hands in exasperation.

"I have been trying to tell you, but that thick skull of yours has left you cork-brained! That agent—"

But whatever James would have said was forestalled by

the circumstance of a knock on the door and the intrusion of his apologetic butler.

"Pardon me, my lord, but you have visitors," he began. "I have put them in the parlor, but if I do say so, I do not think they will . . . stay put."

His prophecy was proven accurate that very moment when a feminine voice was heard to emanate from the hall.

"Denham, I simply refuse to be put in some stuffy parlor that looks as though no one has sat in it for years! I know James is a prisoner of his study, and I have not time to wait until it can be ascertained whether it is possible to lure him from his lair!"

Nicholas felt his heart lurch as he recognized the voice, and in a flash she stood before him in the study, a startling portrait of elegance, beauty, and sophistication. Beside her was her handsome patient, although he was dressed rather better than when Nicholas had seen him last, having, it appeared, the benefit of a visit to Weston's. Nor, Nicholas reflected in irritation, did he look at all in ill health at the moment.

"The Countess of Pembroke . . . and Lord Linden," Denham intoned belatedly.

It is doubtful that any of Denham's stentorian announcements had ever received such a reaction. Comprehension of Robert Westlake's identity slowly filtered through Nicholas's brain, and he remained rooted to the spot in stunned silence. Juliana was equally paralyzed at the sight of her husband's frozen features. Robert was observing his sister's reaction in alarm, and James merely studied the group with an interested smile. Then he made his announcement.

"What fortunate circumstance that we are reunited at last!" he exclaimed. "A toast all around! For now I can share with you a great piece of news that will make you all rejoice!"

He filled the glasses and passed them to his stricken guests, raising his own.

"Napoleon is in retreat from Leipzig!" he exulted. "We have won a great battle, with no small contribution made by the people in this very room. Let us drink to the tyrant's downfall!"

There was a silence. Then Robert spoke.

"I say, that is capital!" he said, and raised his glass jubilantly. "Here, here!"

Nicholas and Juliana looked at each other. Slowly they raised their glasses.

"Here, here!" they said in unison.

The clip-clop of the horses' hooves echoed on the cobblestones as the carriage bearing Nicholas and Juliana made its way to Brook Street. The afternoon weather had taken a decidedly inferior turn, the fog having rolled in and brought with it the beginnings of a steady drizzle. The weather inside the carriage was no better, the two passengers sitting in a pensive and uncomfortable silence underscored by the gloom that filtered in through the windows.

Juliana wished she had Robert by her side for support, but he had, after greeting Nicholas in a most cordial manner, remembered a pressing appointment at his club. James, too, had quickly recalled another engagement. With deep regret he had ushered them outside, where it was only too clear that the service of Nicholas's carriage would be needed if they were both to stay dry. Nicholas's polite inquiry as to where he might drop Juliana was met by her riveting news that she was staying at his house.

And so the carriage rolled on to Brook Street, neither of its occupants having any particular reason to hope that the evening held more promise than the afternoon. Both Juliana and Nicholas were preoccupied with their own thoughts, and neither seemed able to broach the subjects very much on their minds.

To Juliana her husband's silence conveyed utter disapproval of her presence, and she was much dismayed and discouraged, finding herself momentarily at a loss as to how to begin. Nicholas's thoughts, however, were running in an entirely different direction.

"Juliana," he began finally, "I find myself very much the fool once again, having wronged you by the misimpression of your brother's identity. It seems I was all too eager to believe your affections engaged by another."

Juliana ventured a sidelong look at his troubled countenance.

"Truly I am to blame, my lord, for planting the seed," she said. "For you will recall, I told you before we were wed that another claimed my heart. I was but trying to get you to cry off, my lord, and did not mean the literal truth of it. Although I suppose I was attempting somehow to convey the depths of my commitment to finishing this business with James and my brother. Perhaps if I had been honest at the beginning, we would not have had these misunderstandings."

Nicholas shook his head.

"Nay, for I think I would have found a way to believe the worst in any event," he said. "I have been blinded by false appearances since the time I first laid eyes on you, much like that cursed fellow in the play we saw in Pevensey. I was no better than he, accusing his betrothed of unfaithfulness, only I compounded my error by my own unfaithfulness."

"My lord?" Juliana asked, puzzled, although her heart lurched at the thought of him with another woman.

"My search for another woman while wed to you can only be viewed thus," he said quietly.

Juliana gave a gasp that lay somewhere between relief and protest.

"My lord, 'twas my doing! One can only see what is before one, after all, and I was at great pains to show you a false image," Juliana said in agitation. She did not like the turn of this conversation. His regretful apology was beginning to sound like a farewell speech.

Nicholas turned and faced her directly, taking in the emerald eyes that shimmered with a trace of tears, the quivering lips, and the rich auburn tresses that so gently framed her face.

"Juliana, I have only myself to blame for not seeing what was before mine own eyes," he said with a sad smile.

The carriage had pulled up to the house, making further conversation impossible. Nicholas helped Juliana down and then escorted her to the door. She opened her mouth to speak, but he shook his head.

"I shall see you at dinner, my lady," he said formally. Bowing, he turned and walked off in the rain.

Juliana was beside herself in the hours before dinner. She tried to rest but found that thoughts of Nicholas intruded such that she finally got up in disgust.

"What are you, Juliana, some sort of hen-hearted miss without a streak of gumption?" she said aloud as she paced the room. "You are acting the veriest fool! Upon my honor, it is though you never in your life faced down a difficulty!"

With that she summoned her maid and began to dress for dinner. She would show her husband that she could not be dismissed so easily.

But when she faced Nicholas across the table, Juliana found she could manage to say nothing of substance. Between the footmen and the butler and her husband's closed expression, Juliana judged it impossible to open such a conversation as she meant to have that night. And so they spoke of the weather (in London, Sussex, and Yorkshire), the emperor's imminent containment, Mr. Betty's performance as Alexander at Covent Garden, and various other tidbits of interest to neither party.

When Nicholas joined Juliana after dinner, for he did not linger over his port, she fared little better. Nicholas forestalled Juliana's speech by one of his own.

"Juliana, I have given considerable thought to our situation. Indeed, I have thought of little else for weeks," he said, as she looked up at him with the dread of one fully expecting to hear the worst.

"Since our marriage was undertaken under false circumstances, I propose we abandon our arrangement," he said. "You married me out of desperation at the choice put to you by your aunt. I thought to offer you a better choice, but that has brought nothing but pain for both of us."

Juliana opened her mouth to speak, but Nicholas put a hand up to stop her.

"Nay, I must finish, Juliana," he said. "I own, to my great embarrassment, that I was happy with our . . . arrangement while in the throes of my obsession for the woman I believed to be a spy. But somehow as the weeks went on, her image faded, and I realized that I did not find the reality of our marriage . . . at all unpleasant."

He paused to look at her steadily.

"By the time I discovered that you had lied about your visit to Mrs. Duville's, I had come to care for you more than I thought. I shall always regret having lost my temper that night, but I shall never regret what followed."

Juliana blushed.

"Nicholas, I . . ." she began.

He put a finger against her lips and smiled wryly.

"If only I had realized then what I know now, I should not have lost you. But I have never been a student of human relations, my dear, only of words and ideas. I made a thorough muddle of it all. When I believed you preferred another, I thought to do the noble thing and allow you to have him. But I left Yorkshire because I found that I was not the noble sort. I thought to fight for you, somehow—and what folly that was, since 'twas your own brother I believed to be my competition!"

Nicholas gave a bitter laugh.

"I am filled with disgust, Juliana, at the way I have allowed my own emotions to play me false," he said. "You do not deserve to be trapped in this abominable marriage, and I will not allow it. You shall have your independence. I am arranging for an annulment on grounds that your brother did not consent to the marriage. I talked to your brother about it this afternoon, and he has promised to do everything to insure your happiness. You will, of course, be handsomely provided for."

"That is absurd, Nicholas!" Juliana found her tongue at last. "I am of age and need no man's permission to wed!"

He dismissed her objection with a wave of his hand.

"That is not an overwhelming difficulty, Juliana. As your brother was absent when you came of age and you wed when he was still out of the country—in the service of the king, I might add—Robert believes his petition will not be rejected. He is not without influence, Juliana, and the government owes him a great debt. He will make discreet inquiries about the matter tomorrow, and if that strategy does not succeed, I daresay we can find someone who will be willing to say he had a prior promise for your hand."

He paused as an inspiration flew into his brain. The idea brought a twinkle to his eye. "I have always said James has been a bachelor too long for his own good!"

Juliana gave a cry of outrage, but he quickly put his fingers to her lips.

"Don't worry, Juliana. It is the least James can do for you, after all he has put you through, and I am persuaded he will be all too happy to allow you to cry off after this is resolved."

With that he lifted her hand to his lips. The twinkle was gone now.

"I am sorry, my lady spy, to have been the cause of so much distress," he said, looking into her eyes, the pain clear in his own. "I shall move out first thing in the morning, Juliana."

Then he turned and left the room. Juliana remained motionless in her chair.

Juliana had crossed her room for the fiftieth time when
she heard the hour sound midnight. Why was she always
allowing her husband to walk out in some misapprehension
or another? This was truly absurd. He had allowed her no
chance to speak—but there was no reason why she could not
have demanded that he listen to her. She sighed. What had
kept her silent? Was it her fear that he did not want her?

But surely, her heart told her, there was a chance that
he did.

"I cared for you more than I thought." That had been the
only clue to his feelings. No, there was more, Juliana knew.
He said he had thought at one point to fight for her. Abruptly
Juliana shook her head. What did it matter? It was time she
proved she was no coward. After all, all she had to lose was
her husband.

Juliana squared her shoulders and picked up a flannel robe,
wrapping it securely around her flimsy gown. She opened
the door to her chamber, then stopped for a moment at the
threshold. Looking down at the wispy folds of gossamer that
peeked out from under the heavy wrapper, she smiled. And
discarded the robe in a heap at the door.

19

Prince, thou art sad; get thee a wife, get
thee a wife.
—SHAKESPEARE, *Much Ado About Nothing*

JULIANA PUT HER hand on the door to her husband's chamber and gave it a slight push. It opened freely, and she walked into darkness illuminated by what little moonlight filtered in the windows through the fog. Juliana felt a gentle breeze ripple the folds of her gown. She shivered but knew it was not from the cold. Her eyes found the massive bed that occupied the end of the room nearest the windows. Abruptly she gave a cry of frustration. There was no one there!

A deep voice at her elbow nearly surprised her into a shriek.

"Juliana," Nicholas said quietly.

She turned and found her eyes level with his bare chest, which was exposed by the dressing gown he had wrapped only lightly around him.

"May I be of service?" he said, his voice carrying just the hint of a caress.

"I thought to speak to you, my lord," she said, cringing at how oddly formal the words sounded in the present setting.

Nicholas took in his wife's appearance, his eyes moving from her tousled auburn hair to linger on the creamy skin exposed by the deep neckline of her gown and the curves outlined by the tantalizing drape of the sheer fabric. He watched her breasts rise with her uneven breathing. Finally his eyes returned to study her face with frank curiosity.

"I confess that speech is not what comes to my mind at the moment, Juliana, but I desire you to say what is troubling you," he said with a sigh.

Juliana took a deep breath and looked directly into his blue-grey eyes.

"Nicholas, I deeply appreciate your offer tonight of my independence, but—" she began, only to have him interrupt her.

"I know what is troubling you, Juliana, and I should have made myself more plain," he said brusquely.

He turned away from her, and his voice now carried a rough edge that cut through the darkness.

"When I spoke of your being well provided for, I should have perhaps gone into greater detail," he said harshly. "You will have no reason, my lady, to worry about your finances or your cursed personal independence. I have arranged for the precise sum of . . ."

"Damnation, drat, and bother, Nicholas! I do not want my independence!" she cried. "Will you but listen to me for once instead of deciding for yourself what it is that I need?"

Nicholas turned to her, his eyebrows elevated in surprise, his mood clearly deteriorating. He crossed his arms on his chest and looked down at her with what might have been a scowl.

"You have my undivided attention, Juliana," he said coolly. "Pray continue."

"Thank you, I shall!" she said, and began to pace in agitation.

Finally she looked up, her neck craning with the effort of taking in his great height.

"This is no good, Nicholas, pray, come over here," she said, half-pulling and pushing him over to the bed.

"Sit down," she commanded. He sent her a look of long-suffering exasperation but complied without objection. She stood before him, arms akimbo. Sparks shot from her eyes.

"You may believe me the biggest fool in England, but if you think you can leave this house without the spectacle of your poor hysterical wife clinging to you in protest before all of London, you are a greater fool than I!"

In the deafening silence that followed this rather unexpected statement, Nicholas's brow furrowed as he gave the flustered beauty before him the profound consideration he usually reserved for his most demanding texts. He saw, however, that Juliana was not yet done.

"You are full of your pretty speeches, my lord, but never once do you ask me what I want!" she cried. "Had you done so, you would have found the veriest objection to your plan. For I have no more wish to end this marriage than I have to set eyes again on that godforsaken French tavern!"

Her words hung in the air for a moment; neither of them spoke. Nicholas stroked his chin thoughtfully as she stood defiantly before him.

"Why ever not?" he asked gravely, his eyes—had she but studied them—evincing the barest hint of a twinkle.

But Juliana was much consumed by her own discomposed state, and she moved to sit beside him on the bed, her own eyes fixed resolutely ahead. Abruptly she turned to clutch his hand and began to speak with great earnestness.

"Nicholas, do you remember at Lindenwood when you talked about the woman you hoped to marry someday? You said you wanted someone to share your life, your love of learning, and your vision of the world. Someone who _ wanted you . . ." Here, she stopped, unable to bring herself to say the words as he had then, "in bed."

He smiled wistfully.

"I did not think you had remembered that conversation," he responded quietly.

"I have never forgotten it."

They stared at each other. His arm reached for her, but she stayed it.

"What I mean to say, Nicholas, is that I want to be that woman, if you will have me," Juliana explained, looking deeply into his eyes, afraid to guess what they held. Hesitating, she took a deep breath and plunged on.

"Do you understand plain speaking, sir? I want nothing so much as to be your wife, for I do love you dearly."

The pewter eyes caught fire then, and his mouth curved in a gentle smile.

"And I you, Juliana," he said softly.

Juliana stared. Had she heard him aright? She decided she had. Her brow cleared, and she gave a great whoop of joy. Abruptly she stilled.

"Then there is no reason for you to leave, is there, Nicholas? For I shall be driven to distraction if you do!" Her mouth trembled in agitation.

Nicholas placed his fingers under her chin and lifted it slightly.

"My dear, I intend to drive you to distraction, but not precisely in that manner," he said in a hoarse voice, as he brought his mouth down upon hers.

Later, as they lay entwined in each other's arms, Juliana sighed in contentment as she gazed out the window. She nudged Nicholas, who was softly caressing her breast with his fingertip.

"Look, Nicholas, the fog has lifted, and you can see the moon clearly now," she said.

Suddenly with a mischievous smile she propped herself up on her elbow and looked down at him.

"The English moon, you know, is the most beautiful sight in the world," she said provocatively.

Nicholas grinned, for he had not forgotten their old code, but he shook his head.

"No, Juliana, you are," he said, and reached out his arms to pull her down.